Murder on Quadra Island

Sharon McGregor

Whimsical Publications, LLC

Florida

To purchase the authorized electronic edition of *Murder on Quadra Island*,
visit
www.whimsicalpublications.com

Cover art by Janet Durbin
Editing by Brieanna Robertson

ISBN-13: 978-1-63495-038-1

Published by
Whimsical Publications, LLC
Florida

"Well, I did it," she said without preamble. "Not that it did much good."

"Did what?" Abby's mind hadn't made the leap yet from lesson plans to Summer.

"Contacted the police about Patsy."

"What did they say?"

"Not much of anything. They merely said they'd make a note of it, asked for a photo, which I didn't have, and insinuated that since she was a grown woman, I should mind my own business."

"They didn't say that!"

"Well, no," admitted Patsy. "But that's the feeling I came away with. Could you come over?"

"I guess so. For anything in particular?"

"When they asked for a photo, I didn't have one. Patsy wouldn't let anyone take her picture. I took one of Peaches once, sitting on the wall, and she made me delete it because she was in it. I thought maybe if we checked her house more we could find one to give them."

"You're losing your squeamishness about invading her privacy?"

"Yes." Abby could picture Summer at the other end of the phone, biting her lower lip in concentration in the way she had always done when faced with decisions she didn't want to make.

"'I'll be right over. We can housebreak together."

"It's not funny, Abby." Summer's voice was acid. "Privacy is everyone's right and I don't like invading Patsy's."

When Abby arrived, Summer was at the door, key in hand. "I have to check on Peaches anyhow," she said, appearing happy to have an excuse.

They were met by a stretching, sleepy Peaches, who perked up quickly when she heard the can opener. Cat fed, Summer and Abby looked around. "Where do we start?" asked Abby.

"Probably upstairs. People usually keep personal items in their bedrooms."

Patsy's bedroom was spare in decor. Pale blue walls, a plain bedstead with a solid grey duvet as cover and pillow shams to match. A watercolor hung on one wall—a calendar on another. The calendar was from Ace Movers, a national company with a local outlet. A local number had been stamped over the toll-free. "Do you think she brought that home from work? You said you thought she was a dispatcher."

"It's worth a call."

Abby took out her cell and punched in the number. It was answered with a typical greeting on the first ring. "Ace Movers. How may I help you?"

"Could I speak to Patsy, please?" Abby was suddenly aware Summer had never given her Patsy's last name, but how many Patsys could there be in a small office?

"I'm sorry, she's not here." Abby could hear a crackle, as though a hand had been placed over the phone, followed by a murmur of voices. The voice returned to inquire. "Are you a friend of Patsy's?"

"A neighbor, actually. I wanted to get in touch with her."

"So do we," replied the voice. Another muffled consultation took place in the background. "If you do get in touch with her, tell her to call us ASAP. Otherwise, she can pick up her final check in two weeks." With that ultimatum, the conversation ended.

"Well, we now know where she works. Or did work, by the sound of things."

Abby wandered to the closet and flicked through the meager offerings. Patsy didn't spend a lot on her wardrobe, but then she apparently didn't have much of a social life. She stopped at a shirt, a work shirt because it had Ace Movers embroidered on the left shoulder. On the other side was a name tag. Complete with picture. Jackpot!

"Abby, look here." Summer's voice came almost as a whisper. She picked up a newspaper from the bedside table. Patsy certainly read a lot of papers. Or didn't get around to throwing them out. "This is an old one. It's from nearly four years ago. Why would she keep it?"

"Hoarder?" suggested Abby.

"I don't think so. It's folded over to this story. Actually, the rest of the paper is gone, except for this sheet."

She held the paper so both could see. The headline read, *"Martindale convicted of Manslaughter."* The story went on, *"Douglas Martindale has been found guilty of manslaughter in the death of his wife, Laura. Sentencing will follow tomorrow. The body of Laura Martindale was found in the backyard of their Winston Heights home..."*

Other Books by Sharon McGregor

Mystery

The Island Series
Island Charms
Murder at the Island Spa

The Boarding Kennel Series

Old Shadows, New Murder
Murder Is Handy

Chapter One

Douglas pulled aside the curtains and peered out at a steady drizzle. The scene from his front window was beginning to look familiar again after four years. The living room felt foreign to him, though, still covered with the lives of strangers who had rented the house and left behind a patina of their existence.

He needed fresh air. Somewhere in the attic was a box with gumboots and a waterproof jacket. He didn't feel like searching, but he didn't feel like getting soaked either. He climbed the ladder and pulled the switch. No light. He fetched a flashlight. At least that meant the renters hadn't been rooting around in the attic, but he thought of the elderly couple who had lived here, and decided they weren't likely to.

He found a formidable stack of boxes and almost aborted his plan, but one to the side was marked in his own hand—"back closet." The outerwear would be in that. It only took a moment to pull the necessary jacket and boots from the box. When he pulled the boots to dislodge them, they plopped out, with the handle of a black purse wrapped around them. He stared at it for a moment. Laura's purse. Or one of them. She'd kept handbags scattered in every closet in the house. He had bundled up everything haphazardly into boxes to store in the attic, the house readied for renters. Someday, he would need to go through Laura's things, but he wasn't ready yet. He picked up the purse to return it and noticed the end of a letter protruding from a side sleeve.

With only a short hesitation, he pulled the letter from the pouch and stared at the envelope. Mrs. Blanche Covington was printed above the address in Laura's unmistakable block lettering. He turned it over and stared at it. Sealed and stamped, but not posted. Why?

He carried it downstairs with the boots and jacket and sat at the kitchen table, twisting the letter around in his hands. He had three choices, he thought. He could open it and read it. After all, no one would know or care. But he didn't feel up to delving back into Laura's life yet. He could simply discard or burn it. Or he could deliver it to the intended recipient. The last choice gave him a brief flash of amusement. He pictured himself handing a lost letter to Blanche. She'd spit in his face. He sighed and stood up. The best answer was the easiest. Just do with the letter what was originally intended. It was stamped and ready to mail, so he'd mail it.

He felt a flutter of guilt at the pain Blanche would feel when she saw the writing of her dead daughter, but maybe she would get some comfort from the contents. He didn't really care. He didn't owe Blanche anything.

He posted the letter and walked for an hour. When he got back, he took a bottle from the cupboard and poured a healthy shot into a tumbler. Back in a comfortable chair, he picked up the land line. Time to call Jenny. Just as he was about to punch in the numbers, it rang. He looked at the display. It wasn't Jenny's number. Who else knew he was back? Probably some reporter following up the old case. He decided to ignore the phone.

The letter he'd mailed reminded him of the envelope he'd found in his pocket yesterday. His first thought had been that it was an old letter that had been in his jacket when he went in. Now he wasn't so sure. He reached for the jacket he'd been wearing to have another look. He turned all the pockets inside out, but couldn't find any sign of it. He thought back to his bus ride home. He'd laid the jacket on the seat beside him—he remembered that. When he left the bus, he'd grabbed his jacket just as the bus lurched to a stop, nearly making him lose his footing. The letter must have fallen out then.

He shrugged. It wasn't his letter anyhow. But an uneasy feeling began to creep up the back of his neck. If it wasn't his, then who did it belong to, and why did it end up in his jacket? He thought back to his release into freedom. Last thing that happened to him was on the way to the door that was going to send him back to his life. He'd already been handed his possessions and officially released. He remembered bumping into Jack, the trustee who mopped the hallways. He stiffened. He hadn't bumped into Jack. Jack had bumped into him. The envelope had been deliberately placed in his pocket.

Douglas wished his curiosity bug had been a little stronger. If he'd checked the contents when he discovered the envelope, he might not have this feeling of impending doom settling in his stomach. The telephone shrilled again.

Chapter Two

Mandy took a slow pirouette around the room, taking in the new furniture and the still unpacked boxes forming a barricade in front of the door. An orange tabby cat sat perched on the topmost one, switching his tail in short angry sweeps.

She shook her head with a smile and said, "Mom, you never cease to amaze me. I really thought all your talk about moving back to the island was just that—talk. Now, here you are. Just look at this."

Abby dropped her cleaning cloth and furniture polish bottle on the coffee table and perched on the end of it. "I know what you mean. I'm still a little bit in awe of it myself. I've been thinking for years about making changes ever since your father and I..." She glanced at Mandy as her sentence trailed off.

"It's all right, Mom. Matthew and I have quite accepted that you and Dad aren't going to reconcile. I will admit, for the first couple of years, we had hopes."

"The only thing that stopped me from moving back here was the house. I didn't want to get rid of it. After all, it's where you and Matthew grew up, sort of your birthright."

"*That's* why you decided not to sell. And that's why you left all the furniture behind when Max and Dora rented it. Don't let it stop you, Mom. Neither Matthew nor I have any plans to settle the old homestead. And here I thought you decided to rent because you had cold feet. Of course," Mandy went on, sitting across from her mother on the new green and blue loveseat, aiming at catching her eyes directly. "I also wondered if Neil had anything to do with it."

"Ouch," said Abby. "I've been avoiding that sort of introspection. But you could be right. It might have played a minor role—and I do stress the minor—in my decision."

Abby would prefer to drop the subject of Neil, but she knew it was an issue she had to face eventually. She stood, avoiding Mandy's inquiring and concerned look, picked up her cloth, and took a few swipes at the already shining table, then said, "It was never meant to be for the long haul, I guess. Neil and I lived hundreds of miles apart. It's difficult at the best of times maintaining a long distance relationship. And we didn't have the best of times. Maybe we were both going through a mid-life crisis. Anyhow, it's over now and, if we can change the subject, I'm ready for coffee." *Now I'm spouting clichés. But that's what clichés are for, isn't it? To grab at when you don't want to think too hard about something.*

Mandy looked doubtfully at the boxes. "I'll see if I can find the coffee maker."

"Not here," said Abby. "I meant grab a muffin and double-double at Timmies." She jumped up from her perch on the end of the coffee table and took a rueful tug at her jeans' waistband. Abby knew she wouldn't exactly be described as chubby, but the word svelte would certainly not come to mind either when a stranger greeted her. "Maybe a black coffee and a salad somewhere would be better."

"Nope," said Mandy. "We'll go with your first choice. You can start your health kick after I leave." Mandy, at twenty-one, had a metabolism that didn't let her gain an ounce even when she was cramming for exams and living on junk food. Abby hoped she'd stay that way. Hopefully, her lean frame was an inheritance from Richard.

She didn't argue with her daughter's decision. A sweet tooth was one of her greatest failings. Maybe in her new home, she could re-invent herself into a healthy-living, diet-conscious new Abby. But not today. She shooed a cranky cat away from the door. "Sorry, Ajax. I know your fur is in an uproar, but you'll get used to it." She stopped to give him a cat treat, but he sniffed it, turned up his nose, and stalked away. "He'll eat it the minute we're out the door," she said, knowing from years of cat raising that he was putting on a show.

Abby pulled the car out of the parking slot reserved for her condo and headed, not downtown, but southward instead. "We'll find some place along the Old Island Highway," she said. "Even if we don't find a Timmies, there should be lots of coffee shops and tea houses. I'd like to see if I still recognize any of the scenery. I know the Bog Rock is still there."

"Just stay on this side of Ultimate Spa," said Mandy. "I have no intention of ever going near that place again."

"It's miles away," said Abby, but she gave a little shudder as she thought of last year's Christmas stay at the spa. Poor Kelly! Such a short and tragic life.

"Tell me about your summer job," said Mandy, steering them both away from bad memories of last Christmas.

Abby was happy to think about something other than Kelly's murder and the near miss she'd had herself. "It's only a term position and part-time, but it will give me some extra income to help pay for my move. I'll still be doing my regular work from home. I haven't taught for years. At least it will be adults I'm instructing at the community college, so motivation won't be such a pressing factor. I'm sort of looking forward to the change, but feel a little scared too." She stopped suddenly, aware she'd been rambling rather than conversing, then, in one of her usual quick topic changes, said, "I talked to Summer before I came. I haven't seen her in years, but she's still on the island."

"Auntie Summer? We used to call her Auntie, I know, and that's how I think of her. I must have been pretty young when I last saw her, but I do remember her. She had really blond hair and wore it tied back. She wore sort of hippie clothing—long skirts and lots of crocheted vests."

"You do have a good memory. Summer was always a bit of the flower child. I imagine she'll have changed a lot. It's been years since I've seen her, but we all wrote those big long letters every Christmas."

"Are you going to look her up?"

"I already did. We talked on the phone and she invited

me over for coffee tomorrow after I drop you off at the airport." She thought for a moment of the fourth member of their old college group and went on. "I'd like to see Jessica again too. She lives in Victoria, so it wouldn't be hard to drive down occasionally."

"Strange, I don't remember her the way I do Summer. I guess I only saw her once or twice when I was young. Is she the one in a wheelchair?"

"Yes. But only recently. She was in a bad accident a couple of years ago. Ever since then, she's shied away from any mention of meeting sometime or getting together."

"Natural, I guess. She doesn't want old friends to see her the way she is now."

"Hmmm. At least Roger, her husband, keeps us up to date on how she's doing. Thank heavens she picked him in the marriage sweepstakes."

Abby spotted a coffee shop on the right side of the road, just past a gas station, and made a quick turn into the parking lot, putting on her signal at the last moment. The driver behind gave a toot on his horn and she responded with an apologetic wave.

Abby selected a cappuccino as a compromise between black and double-double and decided a bran muffin was really a sort of health food. Feeling quite righteous about her choices, she chose a table by a window. Seated and settled, she liberally spread butter on her muffin, sighing happily as she bit into it.

"Now, let's talk about how you're doing. You haven't even mentioned your studies."

"Too busy concentrating on your move, Mom. But tomorrow it will be back to the books. I think I'm doing pretty well. Grades are fine, and of course I have a good rating for my summer work at the vet's back home. I just want to get it over with and start a real job."

"Have you decided where you're going to apply?"

"Not really. I'm looking for a clinic that specializes in small animals. I worked with livestock a lot during the summer, but it's not really first choice. I might have to take whatever I can for my first job, though." Then she looked at Abby and said, "Oh, that's not what you meant, is it? You want to know what part of the country I want to work in."

She took a long draw on her cup as though deep in thought, then said, "I might just try something really off the wall and go to the Maritimes."

Abby sputtered over a fresh mouthful of coffee, nearly choking. "Really? Are you serious about going that far from home?"

Mandy laughed. "That's what you did, isn't it? I'm just going in the other direction."

"It's not the same at all," protested Abby. "If you went back home, your father would be close by. If you came further west, I'd be closer."

"Meaning I still need parental guidance?" said Mandy.

Abby gave her daughter a closer look and realized she was having fun with her. Mandy's face turned back to serious as she said, "I honestly haven't made up my mind. I'm going to put out applications all over the place and see what happens. I've never been to the east coast. I was joking, but now that I think about it, it could be a great place to live."

Abby wisely said nothing. She didn't want Mandy to move that far, but she couldn't really protest since she had just moved three provinces over herself. And Mandy was an adult, perfectly capable of taking care of herself. *Sometimes I think she's more adult than me.*

Abby still needed to pinch herself to believe she'd actually moved back to the island. It wasn't like her to make such sudden decisions, or at least to follow up on them. She often planned unconventional moves, but the fun had always been in the planning. She always knew, deep down, she never intended to follow through. But this time, she had. Strange, when that the first time she'd been back here in years was such an unhappy event last Christmas. It should have put her off.

Maybe Mandy was right. Maybe this move was about Neil. Maybe by putting even more distance between them, she knew she would have the strength to stay away. Because that was the right choice. She and Neil had had a great romance, but there was no future in it. And Abby was ready for a future. Heaven knew her choices in men had been abominably bad in recent years. Her self-image had taken a beating. Richard had been the only right choice. But that had gone wrong too. It had just taken her twenty years to realize it. She sighed and heard over the sound Mandy's voice calling, "Earth to Mother. Are you with me?"

Abby gave a quick laugh. "Sorry. I was wool-gathering. Perils of approaching old age, I guess."

"Nonsense. You're nowhere near old age. I always think of you and Dad as perennial teenagers. "

"Hmm," said Abby. "You may be right. You and Matthew are becoming the adults. We're reverting."

"Now is the time for you, for both of you, to have fun, don't you think? Your chicks have flown the nest; you're free as a bird." Then she giggled. "We're in a cliché mood today, aren't we? But you know what I mean. I'd like to see you and Dad have some fun in your lives. Even if it isn't together."

Abby agreed. A new chapter was about to start in her life. She was going to reconnect with old friends, start a new job, settle in a new house. Neil was going to play no part in it. That decided, she concentrated on hearing more about her daughter's career plans.

The next morning, she was up early to have breakfast with Mandy before driving her to the airport. In honor of the occasion, Mandy accepted her mother's offerings and downed eggs and toast, and even a slice or two of bacon. Normally, her breakfast was a protein smoothie or cottage cheese and fruit. *Now why can't I do that?*

Mandy had her electronic boarding pass ready and only carry-on luggage, so she headed straight for the boarding lounge. No long farewells. Abby gave her a reluctant good-bye with a long hug.

"Study hard," she said. "And be sure to keep in touch. I love you."

"Love you too, Mom. I'll let you know how everything goes, but if you don't hear from me for a couple of days, it will be because I'm in the middle of a project. Don't worry about me." Then she put on a mock frown. "And as for you, take care of yourself. I know what happens to you when you run into old college friends."

"Summer is a far different person from Nikki," Abby said. She thought back to her near miss on a Lake of the Woods Island a year earlier when she had responded to Nikki's cry for help. "I'm sure no one is trying to kill her."

Chapter Three

Jenny answered on the first ring. "I've been waiting for you to call back." He could hear the accusation in her voice.

"I'm sorry. I was going to call earlier. It's taking a while to get used to being here."

"Have you seen anyone?"

He knew who she was referring to and answered, "No."

"You will. I'm sure."

"I found a letter in the attic. In an old purse of Laura's. It was addressed to Blanche."

He knew Jennie assumed he'd read it. That's what she would have done, he thought.

"What was in it?" she asked.

"I didn't open it. I just posted it to Blanche."

"Why ever not? There could have been something important in there."

He hadn't considered that. Strange. He'd spent four years looking for answers and, possibly, he'd just thrown one away. Now that he was here, the answers he was searching for were keeping their distance.

"It was just a letter to her mother."

"And you don't find that significant? Why write a letter? She was in the same city. They both had a phone. They both had e-mail. Why a letter? Unless there was something physical in there besides the letter?"

That's how he should have been thinking. It was the sight of Laura's handwriting that had thrown him.

Jenny abruptly changed the subject. "When are you coming here?"

"In a day or so. I need to make sure everything is right first."

"And be sure no one is watching you."

"That too."

He hung up the phone, feeling unsettled. Usually, Jenny was his calming influence. This time, she'd rattled him. He swore when he thought about how stupid he'd been with the letter. Then he stood and crossed to the window, staring out. Was that blue pick-up there yesterday? He was getting paranoid now.

Chapter Four

Abby slowed to a crawl, examining the house numbers along the street. Why didn't they make the numbers larger? It wasn't so bad now in the daytime, but she could never read them at night. Then she realized she didn't need numbers. Right ahead of her was an exit into a cul de sac with a sign at the entrance, Meadow Lane. The whole cul de sac was one complex of condos, and from the look of the landscaping and the exteriors, it was a good deal pricier than the one she was living in. Summer must be doing all right for herself.

She parked in a visitor slot and found the number she was looking for. Summer answered before she had a chance to let go of the brass door knocker with an elephant motif.

They gave each other a back-patting hug before pulling apart for examination.

"You've changed!" they said in unison. And indeed, Summer looked far different from the slim, long-haired flower child Abby remembered. She should have known better, though. After all, Summer had included family snaps in the Christmas letters. But it was different seeing her in person. The long blonde hair was now short, and even lighter in color, although if that was grey filling in the blanks, it was still an attractive shade. Summer herself seemed shorter, but that must be an optical illusion due to the extra pounds she was wearing. Abby suddenly became conscious of her own wider girth. How much had she changed since college days?

"You look great, though," said Summer. "I think it's just your hair that makes you look different. You used to keep it longer and pulled back. This looks good on you."

Abby had gone all out when she decided to make changes. In addition to moving back to her old home town, she had changed her hairstyle from a down to the shoulders length to a short, wispier cut. She still didn't know if she liked it.

"You look great, too," said Abby as Summer led her into the sunken living room. While she left to bring a refreshment tray from the kitchen, Abby looked around. A tall fireplace running floor to ceiling was the focal point of the room, but surrounding it were large windows pouring in light onto the polished floor. One set of slider windows opened onto a shady deck with more planters around a white wicker set of deck furniture. Huge plants stood on either side of the fireplace. The furniture was upholstered in soft, colored fabric. One large painting dominated the wall area not given over to windows. The whole effect was light and relaxing, the kind of room where you could either sit for a cozy chat or throw an elegant party.

Abby cast her mind back to Summer's last newsletter and tried to picture the words. She remembered her husband Jack had died a few years ago, but couldn't recall any mention of a job or employment. Maybe he died in financial circumstances that left Summer with the option of working or not as she pleased.

She didn't have long to reminisce. Summer deposited a flowered tray on the table. "I thought tea instead of coffee?" she said as she began to pour. "It's a Rooibos tea with mango bits added. I hope you like it." Abby should have known she wouldn't be served anything as ordinary as Earl Gray or Orange Pekoe by Summer.

"How is Jennifer?" asked Abby. "She's taking law, isn't she?"

"Yes." Summer brightened with maternal pride. "She's studying at Harvard." Abby decided whatever Jack had done must have been well-paying if they could send their daughter to Harvard. Then she remembered. Jack had been an investment broker. He must have been one of the lucky ones, or the smart ones, considering the volatile investment profession as of late. "She'll be home for a visit next month. How about Mandy? And Matthew?"

"Mandy's in Saskatoon, studying to be a vet," said Abby with equal pride. "And Matthew is a nurse working for Doctors Without Borders. I don't get to see him as much as I'd like, but Mandy was here helping me move. I put her on a plane back to Saskatoon this morning."

She took a cautious sip of the Rooibos and decided she liked it. A plate held a variety of cookies, all looking homemade. "Rhubarb creams or lemongrass," Summer said.

Abby took a chance on the rhubarb cream. It was good. She took another swallow of her tea and looked up as she heard a soft meow coming from the patio windows. A gray and white cat sat looking in with a wistful expression. Then it lifted one white paw and began to scratch at the frame.

"Peaches," said Summer, going to the door and letting the cat inside. "What are you doing here?" Peaches waltzed in, tail in the air with that proprietary attitude cats had. Then, noticing Abby, it stopped and sat down a few feet away, regarding her with a suspicious glare.

"Oh, you have a cat too," said Abby in that moment of instant bonding between cat owners. "I have an orange tabby, Ajax. But I thought you had allergies. Or did you manage to get over them?"

"It's not my cat," said Summer. "I do still have allergies, but not as bad. I can handle Peaches in small doses. But she's not mine. She belongs to my neighbor, Patsy."

She coaxed Peaches into the kitchen and set down two bowls, adding water to one and something out of a covered container she pulled out of the fridge into the other.

Peaches didn't quibble about her offerings and dived right into the food.

When Summer returned to the living room and sat down wordlessly with a frown on her forehead, Abby said, "Is the cat a problem?"

"Not the cat, but the owner," sighed Summer. "Patsy is my next door neighbor," she began, and then stopped.

"And you don't get along?" prompted Abby. Summer never used to be so reluctant to share details.

"Oh we get along all right. Actually, I never see much of her. She's a bit of a loner—not the type to pop in for a morning coffee or a drink on the patio. It's just that she seems to have disappeared."

"Disappeared?"

"I haven't seen her since day before yesterday."

"Well, maybe she's gone somewhere for a visit. After all, if you're not close friends, she probably wouldn't tell you. Or maybe she's home, just not answering doors. I've had days when I didn't want company."

"If she went away, she wouldn't leave Peaches out. Peaches is an indoor cat, only goes out on the patio. Last time Patsy went away, she gave me her key and asked me to go in and feed her and check her litter box while she was away."

"Maybe she left in a hurry and forgot. Maybe she'll call tonight and ask you to go over."

"No, she dotes on that cat. She'd never go away and leave her outside or without food."

"I hate to say the obvious, but it seems that's just what she did." Then Abby had a different thought. "Unless she's been hurt or taken a fall and couldn't get to a phone. Is she young or old?"

"She's probably about our age, or maybe a little younger. Old enough to be past the flighty behavior, but a little young for the 'I've fallen and I can't get up' stage." Summer jumped up and went to the kitchen, where she pulled a key on a red string from a wall key-holder. "I have Patsy's key," she said. "Last time she told me to keep it in case of an emergency. Do you think this would qualify as an emergency? It's just that Patsy is such a private person. I'd hate to barge in and find her watching television with the blinds pulled. Maybe Peaches just slipped out."

"I don't think Peaches just slipped out," said Abby. "She looks a little too hungry for that."

"I guess we have to check," said Summer, still a little doubtfully. "We can't run the chance she has taken ill."

They went out the patio entrance, sliding the door shut on Peaches, who looked inclined to follow, and slipped down a small lane leading to the next unit. The patio door was held fast from the inside, so they followed around to the end of the complex and circled back to the front door. Summer knocked and called out. Getting no answer, she took a deep breath and inserted the key.

The door opened onto a foyer identical to Summer's. She called out again and they cautiously entered the living room. It was again similar to next door, but decorated in a haphazard style, with tan leather furniture and mismatched accent tables. The walls were filled with groupings of small paintings, all of them nondescript landscapes. They looked as though they might have been purchased as a lot or at a garage sale. Newspapers were stacked on one of the tables. There was no sign of life.

The kitchen was similarly empty, as was the downstairs half bath and laundry. Upstairs, both bedrooms were quiet. They opened doors to the main bathroom and the en-suite. All empty. All tidy.

They turned to face each other. "Well, she's not hurt or ill," said Summer. "Now I just want to get out of here. Imagine if she walked in the door and found us here."

They clattered down the stairs and out the front door, stopping to double check it was locked behind them.

Back in Summer's living room, it all took on an air of the ridiculous and they both began to giggle.

"I feel like we're back in college, and just got away with some bit of mischief," said Abby.

"Me too," said Summer. "What a relief!" Then she plopped down on the sofa and her expression turned serious. "But now that leaves the real question—where is Patsy?"

"You're really concerned, aren't you?"

"If it was another neighbor, I'd think nothing of it. People come and go all the time. Patsy is different. Aside from the time she left me in charge of Peaches overnight, she never goes anywhere."

"Doesn't she work?"

"Well, yes, she heads off to work every day, but she's a creature of habit. Leaves the same time, arrives home the same time, and then stays put. She has no social life that I've seen, no family apparently and no visitors—ever. Well, except for me once or twice when she first moved in. Then I realized she wanted no part of company and I just left her alone."

"It all sounds rather sad," said Abby. "But you're not talking about the sad part. You're really worried something bad has happened."

Abby's mind flashed to a picture of the home they'd just left. "Did you notice in her house, there's not a single photo album or family picture?"

"I didn't have time to think about it, but yes, I guess you're right."

Summer picked up the teapot, began to pour a refill, then made a face when she realized it had cooled while they were on their escapade. She carried it out to the kitchen and plugged the kettle in again, talking over her shoulder as she went. "When we did talk, she never mentioned husband, kids, friends. She always had this furtiveness about her. She jumped at every sound. It was as though she was afraid of something."

"Or somebody," Abby finished. "You think she was hiding from something?"

"I guess. But she can't really be in hiding if she works."

"Do you know where she works? We could see if she's there. Or if they know where she's gone."

"I'm not sure. I think she said she was a dispatcher, but she didn't say who for."

"Could be a taxi company or a transport one." Abby thought it was strange that a woman who worked in such a low-paying job would live in a pricier condo complex, or vice-versa. But, maybe she had another income and only worked to keep busy.

"How long has she lived here?"

"Nearly four years."

"Do you think we should report it to the police?"

Summer sighed. "I thought about it, but what would we say? I haven't seen a neighbor who I'm not close for two days and she never told me she was going away? I don't think they'd give it much credence." Then she got up and called to Peaches. "I'd better take her back home and be sure her food, water, and litter are okay. Coming?" The kettle began to whistle and Summer detoured to unplug it. "We'll have a refill later."

"Of course," said Abby in response to the last question, her curiosity as piqued as her sense of unease. Behavior changes in the young were normal, but in a middle-aged woman, a break in pattern suggested a crisis of some sort. "Maybe she got a letter with bad news," she suggested.

"Bad news these days comes by phone or e-mail, not by letter."

"Did you see a computer? I don't recall a desk anywhere."

"I'm pretty sure she has a laptop. Probably just sticks it away when she's not using it."

They followed the path around to the front this time, Summer holding a squirming Peaches. Either she was enjoying her newfound freedom or just didn't like being held. When Summer deposited her on the floor after closing the door, it was apparent it wasn't the freedom she was after. Peaches immediately sought out her food dish and stood looking from the bare bowl to Summer in expectation. Obviously, the food she had at Summer's only qualified as an appetizer.

As Summer ministered to the cat, Abby strolled around the living room, looking for anything that might be unusual, a difficult task when you didn't know the person. No mail of any kind sat on counters or tables. It looked as though Patsy read a lot of newspapers, or at least kept them. No personal photos showed. The pictures hanging were all the kind you buy to have something on your wall, not for artistic expression.

Then she spotted the laptop on a lower shelf of the coffee table. She pulled it out and booted it up.

"What are you doing?" demanded Summer as she came up behind Abby.

Abby jumped. "Don't sneak up on me like that."

"Guilty conscience? We're here to see if Patsy is all right, not to snoop."

"I'm not snooping. I'm checking to see if she got some bad news and that's what made her take off," answered Abby in a matter-of-fact tone. "We should try to get some answers before deciding to call the police."

"I wasn't ready to call the police," said Summer. "And we can't just go looking into her personal things." She looked over her shoulder towards the windows as though expecting an accusatory Patsy to materialize any minute.

Abby ignored the protests and clicked on the e-mail account. "Do you protect your e-mail with a password?" she asked.

"No, why bother?"

"I don't either, but Patsy does. Which is strange consider-ing the computer itself wasn't locked. It opened right up."

"I think she's just a cautious person. She always struck me as being fearful—of everything."

"If so, there must be a reason. Maybe she has a past that just caught up with her."

"And maybe we should get out of here," said Summer. Abby complied by shutting down the laptop and stowing it away where she found it.

"But the question remains," Abby said, "where is she and why did she leave in such a hurry she forgot about her cat? It doesn't feel right to me. No matter what the problem, I wouldn't forget to look after Ajax."

Summer didn't answer until they were safely back in her living room, attempting to drink cold tea. She slipped out to the kitchen and put the kettle on again, then returned to say after a considering silence, "If she doesn't show up or call by tomorrow, I'm going to go to the police. Then it's up to them to decide how seriously to take it."

Chapter Five

Next morning, Abby woke with that feeling that something momentous had just happened or was about to. She stretched in bed, trying to think what it was, and snatches of her dream came back to her. She'd been on a plane, which in and of itself was enough to stir up fearful thoughts. But in this dream, she was flying across the ocean, in a deserted airplane with a storm flashing outside the window. No wonder she felt strange. Abby's fear of flying was not abating as she got older, no matter what she did to fight it.

Placing her unrest seemed to dismiss it and she had a leisurely breakfast with Ajax on her knee, trying to ambush her meal with a darting paw. She finished with a second cup of coffee and decided today was the day she would begin her new health-conscious self. The poached egg on whole wheat toast she had just polished off was a good start. But she needed to go shopping. Her fridge and cupboards were still empty except for the few things she'd picked earlier for yesterday's breakfast. The trouble with moving was restarting everything from scratch. All the staples you never thought of unless you needed them needed to be stocked.

She decided against a third coffee and sat down in her recliner—she still needed to buy a new desk—with her laptop. Checking her e-mail was the first order of the day. Then she stiffened with her cursor poised over the first on the list. It was from Neil. She hesitated, then hit delete and went on to the rest. She felt quite virtuous about the delete. She was learning how to shake off the past and get on with her life. But a little voice told her she was just postponing things. Before the day was over, she'd be rooting in her deleted folder to bring up the letter.

She made her shopping run, bringing home half a dozen bags from the grocery and shoving the contents into fridge and cupboards. It was true, she thought, that you shouldn't shop on an empty stomach. By going after breakfast, she'd managed to rein in her usual extravagances and concentrate on foods befitting the new Abby.

Shortly after a lunch of salad with nuts and dried fruits drizzled with a vinaigrette dressing, she decided the time had come to finalize her lesson plans. Her first class would be Monday. She worked undisturbed for an hour, except for the odd fleeting thought of jelly doughnuts, when the phone rang. It was Summer.

"Well, I did it," she said without preamble. "Not that it did much good."

"Did what?" Abby's mind hadn't made the leap yet from lesson plans to Summer.

"Contacted the police about Patsy."

"What did they say?"

"Not much of anything. They merely said they'd make a note of it, asked for a photo, which I didn't have, and insinuated that since she was a grown woman, I should mind my own business."

"They didn't say that!"

"Well, no," admitted Patsy. "But that's the feeling I came away with. Could you come over?"

"I guess so. For anything in particular?"

"When they asked for a photo, I didn't have one. Patsy wouldn't let anyone take her picture. I took one of Peaches once, sitting on the wall, and she made me delete it because she was in it. I thought maybe if we checked her house more we could find one to give them."

"You're losing your squeamishness about invading her privacy?"

"Yes." Abby could picture Summer at the other end of the

phone, biting her lower lip in concentration in the way she had always done when faced with decisions she didn't want to make.

"'I'll be right over. We can housebreak together."

"It's not funny, Abby." Summer's voice was acid. "Privacy is everyone's right and I don't like invading Patsy's."

When Abby arrived, Summer was at the door, key in hand. "I have to check on Peaches anyhow," she said, appearing happy to have an excuse.

They were met by a stretching, sleepy Peaches, who perked up quickly when she heard the can opener. Cat fed, Summer and Abby looked around. "Where do we start?" asked Abby.

"Probably upstairs. People usually keep personal items in their bedrooms."

Patsy's bedroom was spare in decor. Pale blue walls, a plain bedstead with a solid grey duvet as cover and pillow shams to match. A watercolor hung on one wall—a calendar on another. The calendar was from Ace Movers, a national company with a local outlet. A local number had been stamped over the toll-free. "Do you think she brought that home from work? You said you thought she was a dispatcher."

"It's worth a call."

Abby took out her cell and punched in the number. It was answered with a typical greeting on the first ring. "Ace Movers. How may I help you?"

"Could I speak to Patsy, please?" Abby was suddenly aware Summer had never given her Patsy's last name, but how many Patsys could there be in a small office?

"I'm sorry, she's not here." Abby could hear a crackle, as though a hand had been placed over the phone, followed by a murmur of voices. The voice returned to inquire. "Are you a friend of Patsy's?"

"A neighbor, actually. I wanted to get in touch with her."

"So do we," replied the voice. Another muffled consultation took place in the background. "If you do get in touch with her, tell her to call us ASAP. Otherwise, she can pick up her final check in two weeks." With that ultimatum, the conversation ended.

"Well, we now know where she works. Or did work, by the sound of things."

Abby wandered to the closet and flicked through the meager offerings. Patsy didn't spend a lot on her wardrobe, but then she apparently didn't have much of a social life. She stopped at a shirt, a work shirt because it had Ace Movers embroidered on the left shoulder. On the other side was a name tag. Complete with picture. Jackpot!

"Abby, look here." Summer's voice came almost as a whisper. She picked up a newspaper from the bedside table. Patsy certainly read a lot of papers. Or didn't get around to throwing them out. "This is an old one. It's from nearly four years ago. Why would she keep it?"

"Hoarder?" suggested Abby.

"I don't think so. It's folded over to this story. Actually, the rest of the paper is gone, except for this sheet."

She held the paper so both could see. The headline read, "*Martindale convicted of Manslaughter.*" The story went on, "*Douglas Martindale has been found guilty of manslaughter in the death of his wife, Laura. Sentencing will follow tomorrow. The body of Laura Martindale was found in the backyard of their Winston Heights home...*"

"Look at the picture," said Summer, pointing at the caption. Martindale with Laura, and sister, Jenny Dickson, in happier times. "The sister, Jenny, she looks like Patsy, except for the hair."

Abby held the name tag photo close. "Do you think it could be her?"

"Why would she keep it if it wasn't personal in some way?"

Abby shrugged. "Some people collect murder memorabilia. Some people write to convicts. Who knows why? But, you're right; it does look like her." She handed the photo tag to Summer. "I'm going to see what I can find on the Internet about the death. If I can't find anything there, I can check the library. Can you think of anyone she knew besides you?"

Summer wrinkled her brow and said, "I remember once she said something about going to church. I think it was an Anglican one."

"Okay. We'll check the phone books for lists of churches."

"No need," said Summer. "I remember now which one. It was down in the south end of town and I can't remember the name, but I have something better. I have a friend who goes to that church—well, sometimes. I don't think she's a regular. But, I'll take this picture and see if she can tell us anything about Patsy-Jenny."

"What about the police?" asked Abby.

"I told you about that yesterday," said Summer, regarding Abby as though she thought her mind had slipped a cog. "They weren't interested."

"No, I mean the picture. You said they asked for one and you didn't have one. Do you think we should get a copy made of that and give it to them?"

"I have a program on my computer. And I have photo copy paper, so I'll see if I can get a decent copy to keep. Then we can give them this. Now, let's get back home. I'm going to call Melody."

Peaches ignored them as they left. Once in the door, Summer went immediately to the phone on her side table and looked crossly at the receiver. "I'll be so glad to get my cell phone back."

"Did you lose it?"

"No, just dropped it and cracked the case. I found a place I thought was cheap to replace it and they said it would be ready next day. They've had it for three days. I'll get it tomorrow if it's ready or not. A life lesson, I guess—cheap isn't always the best route."

Feeling dismissed, Abby headed home to do her part.

Chapter Six

Douglas opened the front door and scanned the street both ways before stepping over the threshold. He locked the door behind him and picked up a small travel bag. The street was empty, and he turned left, walking with a purposeful gait. Two blocks over, he turned right and passed a cafe and a liquor store before reaching a pharmacy. He stopped just inside the door and pulled out his phone. He scanned the aisles, and, assuring himself the shoppers within view were harmless, punched in a number. Told the taxi would be there in a few minutes, he browsed the shelves, keeping one eye on the street and the traffic, both foot and wheeled. He had no intention of spending another minute in this town.

Nothing aroused his suspicions, so he confidently entered the cab and gave directions to the bus station. He couldn't wait to see Jenny. He tried to remember if she had a car. If not, he could rent one when he got to town. Then he remembered the endless paperwork involved in rentals and decided against it.

Chapter Seven

Abby poured a cup of leftover morning coffee and nuked it in the microwave. One exploratory sip and she dumped it in the sink. She considered making a fresh pot, but decided to get immersed in her searching instead. She googled the names from the newspaper story and found tidbits of information, but nothing seemed to match what she'd just read. She'd try the library next and dig up the old papers from four years ago. They would be stored on microfiche.

The afternoon sun had heated her car past the point of comfort, and the steering wheel was warm and squishy to the touch. She wished enclosed parking was a perk of the condo offerings. Maybe if she decided to sell the Manitoba house and buy a property here, she'd find one with underground parking. But she wasn't going to think about making momentous decisions yet. She wanted to talk to Matthew first and have another conversation with Mandy to be sure they wouldn't miss the old home. Plus, she wasn't sure she was ready to set fire to her own bridges yet.

The Mazda's air conditioning had barely begun to make driving tolerable when she pulled into the library parking lot.

She found a cooperative library assistant to direct her to the old newspapers and give her instructions on how to operate the microfiche. By the time she'd located the right issues, her back and eyes were sore. She scribbled down notes on the steno pad that she always carried in her purse.

It appeared Laura Martindale had been bludgeoned to death and left in the back yard of her home. Her husband had found her and called the police. It didn't take them long to switch their view of husband Douglas from grieving widower to number one suspect. After all, it was usually the spouse or someone else close to the victim. Douglas was tried and convicted of manslaughter, not murder, as it was considered a crime of convenience and passion rather than planning. Douglas protested his innocence, it was noted, but Abby couldn't remember ever reading about killers who didn't.

So. It sounded as though Jenny/Patsy had left home and changed her name. By the dates given, probably right after the trial. Did she fear her brother too? But then, surely she would be safe while he was in prison. Maybe she only wanted to escape publicity. But the crime hadn't been a high-profile one. It had made the news for a short time, and then, with the arrest following so quickly, interest waned. So all the pointers said she was afraid of someone or something else.

Abby tried to find information on Douglas and whether he had been released, but she could find no mention. Maybe he was out now and Abby was wrong. Maybe Patsy was fleeing from him after all. She wasn't sure how to find out. Maybe Summer was making better progress.

She looked at the clock, which read five minutes to six, and realized the library was probably about to close. That would explain the hovering attitude of the library assistant.

Abby signed out and slipped into her little Mazda, glad she'd changed from her old gas guzzler when she decided to move. It was easy to park, and led to much happier visits to the gas station.

If you're going to make a change, it might as well be a big one. And that's what she'd done. New home, new car, new job, new hairdo. She stopped there. The one thing she didn't have was a new relationship, or even an old one, it seemed. She felt a prickle of tears and shook them off. What was over was over. She'd go home and permanently delete that email from Neil. The sky had clouded over, and although still over-warm, the car had lost the blistering heat from her drive over. She glanced at her watch; surely she hadn't been in the library that long.

Her cell phone began to ring as she drove down her home street. She stiffened as she always did when she wasn't expecting a call. With a daughter in a different city and a son whose work took him to the world's hot spots, a ringing phone always held the potential of bad news. Abby kept forgetting to activate Bluetooth, so she decided to be responsible and leave the phone till she could stop the car.

It stopped ringing seconds before she pulled to a halt in her assigned parking spot.

She quickly checked the number in case Mandy or Matthew had been the caller, but it was Summer's home phone that showed on the screen. She let out a breath she didn't realize she'd been holding. Summer could wait till she had a chance to go to the bathroom and put the coffee pot on. Maybe a glass of wine was called for instead.

Abby decided on the coffee. She wanted a clear head to think through the information she'd read.

Ajax was beginning to come out of his sulk at the relocation and wrapped himself around her ankles as she concentrated on counting the spoonfuls of coffee she measured into the filter. She knew from experience he wouldn't let her rest until she had given him the attention he deserved, so she sat down in an easy chair, patted her lap in invitation, and stroked a purring orange cat with one hand as she tried to make sense out of her scribbled notes from the library. She reached across to grab her laptop from the side table so she could enter her thoughts. The movement was enough to unsettle Ajax.

He gave her a dirty look and jumped down, stalking off to the stairs. Royalty was not amused.

Cat-bonding session obviously over, Abby poured her coffee and returned Summer's call.

Three rings before she picked up. "Can I call you back in a few minutes? I'm just eating dinner."

Abby glanced at her clock and realized she had totally forgotten about dinner. A very unusual occurrence for her. Maybe that's what she needed to make a diet work, something to concentrate on, like this puzzle of Patsy's disappearance. Then she scolded herself for her flippant reaction to what could be a serious problem. Patsy might be in trouble.

While she waited for Summer to return the call, she made her own supper. Supper, dinner, she never did get the hang of the difference. As a child it had always been lunch and supper. It only became dinner when they had company. Now she used the words interchangeably.

Whatever one called it, she was still on her virtuous diet, so she selected a chicken breast to bake in the oven. She had broccoli and cauliflower, which she mixed for her vegetables. Could she enjoy them without lashings of butter and cheese? She was going to try to find out tonight. Maybe some new mixture of spices would make up for the lack of cheese. But then, her spice cupboard was nearly bare too. It was time to do a proper shopping run, not the hit-and-miss, one meal at a time way she was doing so far.

Her cell rang, and she checked to make sure nothing would ruin while she talked, before taking her phone to the living room to reclaim her coffee. Ajax was still missing in action.

"How did you make out?'" they asked, nearly in unison. Abby plunged in while Summer was giggling the way they used to when they duplicated phrases.

"I found some more about the original death four years ago, but nothing recent about where any of the people are now." She went on to describe what she had read about the discovery of Laura's body and the resultant conviction of Douglas. "I wonder if he's out of jail now?"

"Four years? It doesn't seem a lot for killing your wife."

"It wasn't called a murder. Manslaughter is treated a lot differently, I think. And I've read stories of lots shorter terms for similar deaths. He could easily be released, especially for good behavior if he minded his P's and Q's in prison. And that could explain why Patsy has run off. Maybe she's afraid of him too. Maybe she came here to start a new life while he was in prison and now he's out and she's running away again."

"I don't think so," said Summer.

"Why not?"

"I hate explaining things on the phone," said Summer. "Can you come over and we can talk about it?"

Abby thought about her dinner cooking in the oven and her stomach rumbled. "Why don't you come here instead?" She suggested. That way she could finish her meal while

Summer was on her way over.

"Okay. Just give me your address."

Abby did and ran to rescue her dinner. Then she spotted Ajax coming back down the stairs and remembered Summer's cat allergy. Oh well, it couldn't be life threatening if she could take Peaches in small doses, she thought. She took Ajax back up the stairs and shut him up in the bedroom. He gave a squawk of protest and then silence. He probably wouldn't speak to her for the rest of the night now.

Downstairs, she grabbed a few bites of dinner, enough to stop the hunger pangs. She'd save the rest to eat in peace and quiet after Summer left, so she put it in a covered container in the fridge and threw the dirty dishes in the dishwasher. She took the Swiffer around the laminate floors and thought that probably got rid of most of Ajax's dander and hair. At least they hadn't been there long enough for hosts of allergens to build up in the curtains and upholstery. It was nice enough outside that they could have tea on the patio. The kettle was starting to boil. She'd remembered Summer never drank coffee.

One more stolen bite of chicken from the fridge before the doorbell rang. She swallowed quickly and opened the door to Summer, who stood with a plastic covered container in her hand.

"I thought you probably didn't have time to bake yet, so I brought some treats to go with our tea."

Abby fought between a groan at the thought of refusing extra calories and salivating at the anticipation of the goodies. The goodies were going to win, of course. Abby had never been much of a baker, or a cook for that matter. Richard had been the chef in their family. Abby's meals had always been edible, but ho-hum, which worked well when the kids were young. Children took time to develop experimental palates.

"Come in," said Abby, taking the plate from Summer. They must be fresh. She could smell delicious scents wafting from the plate. "I thought we'd sit on the patio because of Ajax. I forgot about your allergies until I'd hung up. I tried to do a clean-up and I locked Ajax upstairs, but maybe we'd be safest outside?"

"Oh no. I'll be fine for a short while as long as he isn't in the room. I remembered Ajax and took an allergy pill before

I left."

"Well, have a seat and I'll get the tea." She took the container to the kitchen and set the cookies on a plate. Yummy. They had fruit and nuts of some sort in them, she could tell, and they smelled divine. Dieting was definitely on the back burner tonight. She poured the kettle into the teapot and added creamer and sugar pots to the tray.

Summer was looking pleased with herself as Abby set the tray down on the coffee table. They waited a moment for the tea to finish steeping as though in agreement for refreshments to be cared for first. Abby bypassed the sugar. She could take it or leave it in tea. It was coffee that reached out to her and demanded sweetness. Summer added a dollop of milk to hers, stirring it with maddening slowness. By the time she took her first sip, Abby had already demolished one cookie and reached for a second. Summer picked one up and broke it into two equal parts, nibbling gingerly on one half.

Deciding the niceties had been well appreciated and it was time to get down to business, Abby used her finger to tap a few last crumbs from her second cookie and said, "Okay, give. You sounded as though you'd found out something interesting."

Summer set down the second half of the raisin and nut cookie and wiped her fingers on a serviette before answering. "Remember I told you I had a friend who went to the same church as Patsy?"

"Yes. Has she seen her?"

Summer ignored the question, determined to tell her story in her own time. Abby knew from experience it was best to let her. She picked up the teapot and aimed it questioningly in Summer's direction. At her answering nod, she poured a warm up into both cups. She gave a sideways glance at the cookie plate, but enough was enough. She restrained herself from bolting a third one. She thought ruefully about the chicken and broccoli cooling in the fridge.

"Well, I had coffee with Melody this afternoon. I asked her about Patsy and she recognized her from the picture. She says she usually goes to church but always sits in the back and doesn't stop to chat with anyone or belong to any group within the church. She called her a ghost, said she's there but she's not. You know?"

Abby nodded. She'd gone through a brief period in her own life after the breakup of her marriage when she felt like a ghost, ethereal and detached from real life, going through the motions.

Summer continued. "She said Patsy never went to church this past Sunday. She noticed because she's so regular— never misses." She stopped in thought for a moment and went on. "It seems rather strange that, in spite of trying so hard to stay invisible, that's the very thing that made Melody notice her."

"So we're no further ahead if the only person we know who knows her hasn't seen her either." Abby was getting impatient with Summer's progress in the tale.

"Not so fast," said Summer. "I said she hadn't seen her at *church.*"

Abby set her cup down with a clatter "So get on with it. Where and when did she see her? And was she all right?"

"Melody has a daughter who works part-time with the ferries. Melody was dropping her off at work when she saw Patsy walking on to the ferry to Quadra."

"So she's gone off without telling anyone and left her cat to fend for itself. I'm beginning not to like her."

"But she wasn't alone." Summer dropped the words slowly in front of Abby.

Getting the reaction from Abby she was apparently looking for—and here Abby had always thought their friend Nikki was the drama queen of their little college group— Summer said, "She was with a man. He had her by the arm and it looked like he was pushing her along."

"As in abducted?" Abby sat bolt upright. Maybe now was the time to get the police involved. But Summer went on with an unconcerned voice.

"No, or Melody would have called someone. She said it looked as though they were arguing about something, but Patsy was going along under her own steam. Patsy was doing most of the talking. Then they stopped and it was Patsy that led the way onto the ferry."

"They went on as foot passengers?"

"Yes, which is rather strange since usually foot passengers are the residents who leave their cars parked on the other side and walk over. They must have known someone on the other side or had some method of transportation arranged."

"Maybe they were going to use a taxi, or walk. Did she describe the man?"

"Quadra is a little big and too spread out to plan on walking where you want to go." She moved on to question number two. "Melody gave me a general description. He was slim but well built, a head taller than Patsy, light complexion and brown hair, not exactly unique."

"And Patsy didn't look frightened of this man?"

"Melody said she kept looking over her shoulder, so if she was fearful, it wasn't directed at the man she was with. But then Patsy always looked as though she was afraid of her shadow."

"Hmm," was all Abby said.

"So I guess that wraps it up."

"You never dropped the picture at the police station?"

"I didn't see the point. Patsy was alive and well and not in any apparent danger. She just did a flit with some man. Do you think she had a long lost lover?"

"You said they were arguing."

"Well you can argue with a long lost lover. That's usually what makes them long lost. The point is she is safe and well and we no longer have a mystery."

"It still seems funny, though," said Abby. "If I made a rendezvous with an old lover, I'd still remember to call someone about Ajax." That line of thought made her think of the unopened and deleted e-mail from Neil. She mentally shook off that trail of thinking. She intended to keep Neil long lost.

Mystery solved, they moved the conversation on. They spent the rest of the pot of tea talking about college days and early married years.

"Remember Nikki at your wedding?" asked Summer. "She decided to do a little rearranging with the maid of honor dress?"

"It took me a while to forgive her for that," said Abby. "All those fittings and she was little miss mealy-mouth. Then, at the last minute, she had her own seamstress alter the gown till it was practically unrecognizable." She sighed. "I know nobody likes bridesmaid's dresses," she said, "but, usually, you suck it up and wear what the bride dictates. But,

Nikki always did like to dress in her own style. Once I thought about it, I realized she made it look a lot better. What riled me was not telling me. If she'd asked to change it, I would have gone along with it. The bride isn't supposed to be surprised on her wedding day."

"Well, not by her maid of honor," giggled Summer. "We were cross with her too. She could have told us and done the same thing for our dresses."

Abby gave her a cold look. "Are you trying to tell me none of you appreciated my fashion sense?"

"You have to admit, Nikki was the clothes horse in our group."

Abby thought back to her wedding day, remembered how Nikki had remained in her under-slip as she helped Abby dress, then darted off at the last minute to put on her own gown, out from under the bride's gaze. Abby realized what had happened at the last minute as they gathered in the foyer of the church to begin the walk down the aisle. She gave a giggle as she remembered. When she walked to the front of the church, Richard turned to her, to be met by a glowering bride. It hadn't taken long to lose the glower. After all, she was there marrying the man she loved. The feeling of betrayal by Nikki lasted until the punch bowl hit the halfway mark at the reception, then melted away into the love that filled the room. She'd forget all about the incident, then bring out her wedding photos and remember again. She never felt any lasting rancour, only growing amusement over the years. Nikki hadn't changed a bit. She still expected things to go her way, usually brought about by just going ahead and doing things, and telling people later.

"Your wedding had a few high points too," Abby said. "Remember, Jessica ended up with two dates? She invited her boyfriend to come as her escort, not realizing she was expected to spend her time with her opposing groomsman, Roger."

"That turned out all right in the end, too," said Summer. "The boyfriend disappeared and she did marry Roger, eventually."

"She wasn't happy at the time. I remember her sulking till the dancing began. It took Roger a while to win her over, but thank heavens he did. I don't know where she'd be today without him." Abby saddened at the thought of their fourth member of the group, confined for the rest of her life to a wheelchair.

"Have you heard anything from Jessica recently? Her Christmas letters never really say anything." Jessica was always the one, along with Nikki, to initiate their adventures before talking Summer and Abby into their foolishness. *Without them, we wouldn't have had nearly as much fun,* thought Abby.

"She's not in very good shape. The accident left her paralyzed from the waist down. She gets around pretty well in an electric wheelchair, and Roger has someone hired to stay with her in the daytime. I tried to see her the last couple of times I went to Victoria, but she always found an excuse as to why we couldn't meet."

"So sad. In one minute, a hit-and-run driver can change your life forever. I guess there's no hope of reversing the damage?"

"I don't think so." Summer sat in thought for a moment, then said, "Maybe if we go to see her together, she'll agree to see us."

"The best chance is probably to get Roger in on it. I'm sure once we get there, we can get her out and doing something. Maybe a concert."

"I'm in," agreed Summer. She gave a quick glance at her bejewelled watch and said, "Now I've got to be off. Those allergy pills only last so long."

After Summer left, Abby no longer felt hungry. The little bit of chicken dinner she had eaten and the two cookies shouldn't have filled her that much. Did she really feel disappointment that they no longer had a mystery? She should be feeling happy instead of let-down. A woman was alive and well, not kidnapped or hurt or in danger. But she knew her preoccupation was more than that. She had niggling doubts. Something didn't feel right about Patsy's departure, and it wasn't only an abandoned cat. It had more to do with the newspaper stories she'd read.

She had a bath to settle her thoughts. A liberal dose of Barefoot Venus bath salts invited her in for a long soak. She leaned back in the tub, trying to make sense of her notes from the library, but only succeeded in getting them wet.

Disgustedly, she threw them on the bathroom floor and reached for her wineglass that sat balancing precariously on the edge of the tub. She made a face. At some point, she'd managed to float a bubble of flavoured bathwater into the glass and the wine tasted terrible.

Abby gave up on the relaxation bit and toweled off, brushed her teeth, and got ready for bed. She climbed in and pulled the covers up. Ajax padded into the room, jumped on the bed, and lay across her abdomen, kneading his claws into her belly and purring loudly.

She lay in bed thinking for a while, absent-mindedly petting Ajax, who had decided to forgive her for her sins. She stared at the laptop she'd brought to her bedside table and opened her e-mail, clicking on the deleted file. She knew she wouldn't be able to sleep till she'd read whatever Neil had to say.

It was short and sweet. *"I don't think we finished talking, Abby. I know I didn't. Will you call me?"* It was a far different thought than the last one he'd expressed before they parted. She was hazy on the exact words, but both, "You're too wrapped up in your own insecurities to have a relationship," and, "You know you're secretly still in love with your ex-husband," rang a bell.

She sighed and hit delete again, this time finalizing it. Then she logged off, pushed Ajax to the side, and rolled over, determined to sleep. But she couldn't get Neil's comments out of her mind. Not the "we have to talk" sentiment, but the more unsettling parting ones. Was she still secretly in love with her ex? She had thought for years that she and Richard had the perfect marriage, until she discovered that, while Richard loved her in his own way, it didn't stop him from having affairs. Strangely, they had parted amicably, a situation made easier by the fact their children were nearly adults. They were still friends, able to meet without rancour. But secretly in love? No, Neil was wrong there. Disappointment and betrayal had killed any remaining love she felt for Richard. She was certain of that. What remained was friendship and a mutual concern for their children.

On that decisive note, she fell asleep, willing herself not to dream of either man. When she woke, if she did dream, she couldn't remember any of it.

Chapter Eight

Abby had her first classes at the community college the next day. One was at ten o'clock and the other at one.

She ate breakfast on the patio, going over her lesson plans for the day. It had been many years since she had taught an English class, or a class of any sort. The butterflies in her stomach were having a free-for-all. She was second-guessing her decision to do this. She could have managed without the extra money this term position brought in, but it would have meant dipping into RRSPs to fund her move, and she didn't want to deplete what she thought of as her emergency stash. It was only for a few weeks and then she could go back to life as it was, relying on her contracts with education publishers for her daily bread. She would just have to hold her breath and plunge in.

Abby arrived much earlier than she needed to, wandered around the hallways for a while to get used to her surroundings, and took a last minute trip to the washroom. Her first class went off without a hitch. The registered numbers weren't large and there were a couple of absentees to deplete the ranks further. The students who were there seemed willing to listen and give her a chance. As they were mostly adults, she found it easy to relate to them and, before the class was over, discovered she was enjoying herself.

She took lunch in the cafeteria, sitting alone until two other teachers approached and asked to join her. Once they sat down, however, they began a two-way conversation that didn't seem to include her. So she felt free to let her mind drift. When she finished eating and stood up with her tray, they both smiled brightly at her as though they had all been having a cozy lunch together. "So glad to meet a new teacher," said one, and the other murmured assent. Since they had never introduced themselves, Abby left feeling a little like Alice in the Wonderland books. Still, they had seemed welcoming, and she smiled back and wished them the best of days.

She felt much calmer going into her second session.

When she arrived home and gave Ajax the attention he expected, she still felt the tension in her shoulders from her morning worry feast. She ran a bath, adding Ruby Red salts, and sank back against the porcelain, relaxing when it warmed to her body temperature.

She heard her cell phone ringing and scolded herself for not turning it off. How could you relax in the tub knowing someone was calling? She spent another few minutes trying to get comfortable, but couldn't ignore her curiosity. When you had children, it didn't matter how old they were, a ringing telephone always held the possibility of crisis.

She towelled off and dressed quickly, then ran to retrieve her annoying phone. She checked the last number, which said "unknown caller." There was a voice message. "Hi, Abby, it's Summer. I finally got my cell back. Give me a call." Then she added her number, which Abby posted into contacts.

Grumbling under her breath about aborting a bath for nothing, she made a small pot of coffee before returning the call.

"Hi, Summer, what's up?" she said.

"I got my cell phone back this afternoon."

"Yes, you said in the message. Good." Was that all she had called for?

"I had messages."

"I imagine you would," said Abby, wishing she would get on with it. The smell of brewing coffee was calling to her and she poured a cup, balancing the phone between her chin and shoulder.

"One of them was from Patsy."

Abby sat down in a nearby chair with a thump. "When was the message from? And what did she say?"

"You can quit being cross with her for forgetting her cat. She said she got called away suddenly and I could use my key to go in and look after Peaches till she got back. She probably thought I'd get to my cell quicker and didn't realize it was out of my hands."

"Well, that makes everything normal then. Patsy's just a one-off character who decided on the spur of the moment to go away." Then she thought about their call to Ace Movers. "It is strange that she didn't tell her boss she was taking time off."

"Yes. And it doesn't explain her encounter with the man at the ferry and her behavior there."

"Are you still worried about her?"

"A little, but then she's a grown woman and not my responsibility. I feel foolish about contacting the police, though."

"You said they didn't seem interested, so I don't imagine they spent a lot of man hours on it. Still, maybe we should say we've heard from her? We don't want to be accused of wasting police resources, or whatever they call it."

Abby was about to hang up when Summer said, "Just a minute. Someone came up to Patsy's door."

"Maybe a salesman."

"It's a woman." Abby could picture Summer peering through her curtains to the next door residence. "She's not even knocking. She's gone to the flower garden and is peeking in the window. That's rather bizarre. Now she's back at the door, knocking this time. She looks awfully furtive. She's leaving a note!"

"What's furtive about leaving a note? It sounds like quite normal behavior to me. She's probably an old friend from out of town who wants to get in touch."

"Except that Patsy didn't have any old friends. Or at least none she wanted to keep in touch with. She changed her name, remember?" Abby could hear Summer opening a door. "She's gone now. I'm going to check the note."

Before Abby could think of a protest and decided after all she was as curious as Summer, she was back on the line.

"This is really strange."

Abby could hear paper crackling, but Summer had stopped talking.

"Tell me." Abby could hear her voice rising. Summer could be so annoying sometimes. "Just spit it out."

"Okay, I'm just trying to decipher the handwriting. She has quite a scrawl. It says, 'Jenny, I need to talk to you. I have some information for Douglas. If you know where he is, call me.' It's signed Blanche and there's a phone number."

The name struck a note with Abby. It was an unusual one in this generation. "Just a minute." She scrambled through her notes and found what she was looking for. "Here it is, 'Blanche will be Blanche Covington. She's the mother of Laura, Douglas's wife.'"

"Wow." Other than that one word, Summer was uncharacteristically speechless. So was Abby.

"So," said Abby finally, after thinking furiously for a moment. "Should we assume that the man Patsy—I guess we should start calling her Jenny—was with at the ferry was her brother Douglas? Blanche seems to think he's with his sister. But she could be wrong; it might be someone else."

"That means he's out of prison."

"And they're trying to get away from someone."

"Blanche?"

"Maybe. But the note sounds as though she has good news for Douglas. It certainly isn't threatening in any way. I know some men try to avoid their mothers-in-law, but not to that extreme."

"He might not know that, though," said Summer. "He hasn't seen the note. But I can't see why he would be frightened of her. I can't see why he would be frightened of anyone. If he served his time." She stopped suddenly. "You don't suppose he broke out of prison, do you?"

"If he had, it would have been in the news. I think it's safe to assume, if he's out, it's legal. But we don't even know for sure if it *is* him. And he might be frightened of Blanche. Don't forget she was the mother of the woman he killed. That would be reason enough to avoid her. He might worry about her making a public scene, or even physically attacking him."

"Mmm." Summer didn't sound convinced. "I still think there's something strange going on."

"Maybe there is, but it's not our problem. All you have to

do is look after Peaches until Patsy, er Jenny, gets back from her rendezvous. Then all will be back to normal."

"You think so? I don't."

Abby knew from long experience it was no use arguing with Summer when she got a bee in her bonnet, so she said goodnight and went off to feed Ajax before starting her own dinner. She grinned at the thought that Summer was now the inquisitive one and Abby was the restraining voice of reason. Talk about role-reversal.

Chapter Nine

Abby woke to the warm feel of fur draped over half her face. An orange paw attached to the fur was patting her head in a steady rhythm.

"All right, Ajax," she said, rolling out of bed. "I know I'm late this morning with your breakfast."

She needed a shower to wake up properly, but knew Ajax had to be fed first or he'd sit outside the shower door and howl at her.

Abby made the shower a short one—no time for a relaxing bath. She had slept in. Good thing Ajax woke her up. She didn't usually sleep this late and she had a class this morning. It wasn't until ten o'clock, thank goodness.

She was finishing a last cup of coffee and putting her lesson together when the phone rang.

"Summer."

"I hope I didn't wake you up, but I thought you said you had a class this morning."

"I do. I'm on the way out the door now."

"I won't keep you a minute. Do you have other classes today or are you free for lunch? I realized we spent most of our time talking about Patsy and never did get into a good reminisce. We could catch up over lunch."

"Only a morning one today. Where do you want to go?"

"You probably wouldn't recognize the restaurants around now, so is it all right if I select the place and pick you up?"

"Sure. How about one o'clock?" That would give her plenty of time to change after class.

"Can we make it twelve-thirty?"

"Okay. Look, Summer. I have to dash. I'll see you then."

The morning class was a little stressful, as she had one new member who seemed to question every statement anyone made. A good thing in the right dose, but annoying when it became a formula for his input.

She was looking forward to a relaxing lunch and a trip down memory lane.

At home, Ajax was sleeping on the bed and barely glanced at her. He was feeling right at home now. She quickly changed and brushed her hair, barely in time to answer the door.

"I think I need this outing," she said.

"Classes not going well?"

"They've all been good until this morning." She told Summer about her new student. "I'll just have to come up with a method of dealing with him before he drives the whole class nuts. Maybe if I get him to initiate the discussions, he won't tear them apart so much." They drove along the highway beside the ocean, heading north towards downtown. Abby said, "Where are we going? You never said."

"It's called The Unicorn. Strange name but an extensive menu, the food is good, and the atmosphere relaxed." Summer turned off to the right, entering a large paved area.

Abby looked ahead at the sign—BC Ferries. "Summer! You're not taking us on a wild goose chase, are you?"

"Of course not. We're not going to Quadra to look for Patsy—um, Jenny. We're going because it has a terrific restaurant and it will get you away from all this." Summer waved her hand in a general way to include all directions of stress that might remain on Abby's plate. "Then after lunch," she added, "it wouldn't hurt to take a drive around and see the countryside there. It's quite lovely, and will take the kinks out of that overworked worry lobe of your brain."

Abby gave her a suspicious glance, but Summer put on her best innocent expression and stopped at the ferry booth to pass them her card. They drove on and it was only a few minutes before they began to move. Summer must have had this planned down to the minute. *What if I'd been late getting ready?* Abby wondered. *Only a later ferry, I suppose.*

They rolled off at the other side and went up a steep incline before taking a road to the left. It *was* a pretty island, thought Abby. Already the stress was sliding off her shoulders and neck.

A few minutes later, they took another turn and followed that road to a large parking lot with a sign that read The Unicorn. It was a log-faced building that seemed to fit right into the treed surroundings. Large windows covered much of the side wall. Planters holding all sorts of foliage and bloom hung from eaves and stood at corners of the beds, which were full of shrubs. *They must have a full-time gardener*, Abby thought as they rounded the corner to the entrance. A floating walk led down to landscaped yards, with a trellised rose garden and farther down what appeared to be a wildflower bed. Stone benches dotted the area, inviting a stop for peace and tranquility. For one brief moment, it reminded Abby of the spa where they had spent last Christmas. She pushed that image to the back of her mind. It wasn't the route to stress relief.

It looked expensive. And busy, according to the parking lot.

"We don't need a reservation, do we? Or did you make one?"

"Not for lunch." True enough, the place wasn't nearly as full as you would imagine by the number of cars. Maybe people parked here and walked to other destinations.

Although the room was large, it was sectioned into smaller areas by partial walls and planters and a few huge sculptures, giving it a cozy ambience. A fireplace, unlit, reached to the ceiling along the far wall. The stonework echoed the rustic look. Antique brass containers lined the mantle.

They were led to a table for four by a window with a view of more spacious gardens, the opposite side to the area they had seen from the entrance. Raised flower beds, a small ornamental pond, and splendidly-colored shrubs promised a relaxing atmosphere. Unusual stretch of gardens for a restaurant, thought Abby, but then she could see buildings further along. Wooden signposts directed walkers along marked pathways. Maybe they'd have time after lunch to explore whatever else the Unicorn offered. Maybe an artist colony or a—no. *Just concentrate on the gardens and a lovely lunch, Abby.*

Abby set her purse on the chair beside her and settled comfortably into the plush seat. A linen table-covering, cloth napkins in silver engraved rings, and a full complement of cutlery and glasses indicated this would not be an inexpensive lunch. Abby wondered if Summer was a regular guest here and, if so, who her companion would be. They hadn't reached that point in their catch-up.

A waiter arrived with menus for lunch and drinks. Abby selected clam chowder, something she had never found as satisfying on the prairies, and a Mediterranean salad.

"Go ahead and have some wine," said Summer. "You're not driving. I'll have a sparkler substitute. I could chance a glass, but you never know how much it takes to blow over if you're stopped."

Abby took her up on it and ordered a glass of Chardonnay, which arrived promptly.

"So," said Summer. "Tell me all about your adventure with Nikki last summer. The details the two of you gave in your Christmas letter were a little sparse."

Abby gave a little shudder as she remembered the morning she had stared into the barrel of a handgun, been tied up, and then taken on a cross-island trek to her planned demise. It had been a near miss.

She gave Summer a few more details over the chowder, but was anxious to get the spotlight on her friend.

But Summer wasn't finished. "And this lawyer of Nikki's—Neil, I think she said his name was? I gather you two are an item."

"Not anymore," said Abby shortly. "Sorry, Summer, but it worked for a while long distance, then it fizzled to a halt. I don't want to think about it now."

"Okay. Neil is off limits. How about Richard? Do you see much of him? I don't think I've seen him since that bash you had for your anniversary, and I hate to think how many years ago that was. Which one was that? Tenth?"

"Fifteenth," said Abby. "It's the only time we had a big celebration. I'm not sure why. Most people have the big dos for twenty-fifth or some landmark year. We chose the fifteenth."

"I can't believe it was fifteen years."

"Me neither," laughed Abby. "Sometimes it all seems like yesterday. Richard and I are good friends now. Always have been, I guess, in spite of our divorce."

"And you spent last Christmas here without contacting me? I'm hurt." Her smile countered the words.

"It wasn't exactly a visiting sort of trip. Richard came out with his fiancée Kelly for a getaway at the spa and invited Mandy to join them. I came only when Mandy sent me an SOS after Kelly was killed."

"You do have a talent for getting into predicaments."

"And that's why I don't want you leading me into another."

"Me? We aren't anywhere near predicament. We're just trying to find out why my neighbor disappeared suddenly."

"But now you have her message and you know she's all right. So we can let it go." Abby decided to be firm about changing the direction of the conversation. "We do need to have a proper reunion someday," she said. "Now that three of us are living on the Island, we'll have it here. We'll ask Nikki to fly out and we'll find some way to make Jessica join in. That will be Nikki's job. She could always get Jessica to do anything."

Summer didn't reply. Her gaze was on the garden outside their window, but her mind was obviously elsewhere.

"I know we've been saying we have to visit Jessica, but let's make a definite plan," Abby said, ignoring Summer's faraway look. "As soon as Patsy comes home and we know for sure this is all over, let's phone Roger."

Summer's mind was still on its distant journey. "Of course we haven't explained all the sudden visitors."

"All the visitors? What are you talking about? Oh you mean Patsy. Sorry—Jenny," she corrected. She let out a sigh of resignation. Summer wasn't going to let it rest. Abby wondered if she'd even been listening to her about the reunion. "Who else came besides Blanche? And of course the man she went off with?"

"Didn't I tell you about the other man?" Summer's expression flittered from abstracted to coy to a satisfied smirk.

"No." Summer could be so maddening sometimes. "What other man and where did you see him?"

"It was just after Blanche left the note. A man, dressed in jeans and a denim jacket, knocked at the door, but he didn't stay. I think he might have seen me looking out the window. Anyhow, he just knocked and left."

"And you never thought to tell me?"

"Well, it was after we'd talked and you were going to start dinner. I didn't want to ring again. I thought I'd tell you in the morning, but I forgot. I didn't think it was important. He didn't look suspicious at all. I think he was someone from her work checking to see if she was at home."

Abby wondered where Summer drew the line as to what behavior was suspicious and what wasn't. The man knocking at the door surely deserved as much scrutiny as a woman leaving a note. She gave a mental shrug. It was all moot now. It appeared there was nothing wrong with Patsy—she must get used to thinking of her as Jenny— and everyone was entitled to act weird once in a while. She changed the subject again, this time with more success.

"Now it's time to put you in the witness box. Are you working? Do you have anyone in your life? How is Jennifer doing in law school?"

"No to the first question. I volunteer with a few groups, help out with crafts at the Seniors' Center. I manage to keep busy. Jennifer is doing well. She has focus like I never did. I'm sure she gets it from Jack. She has one more year at University, but hasn't told me where she's looking for a position. I'm afraid she's going to stay down there because she has someone in her life now, another potential lawyer. She doesn't talk much about him, so I know it's serious."

"I wish Mandy would find someone. But, then again, maybe she has. You're right about the talking part. They tell you everything about the casual affairs. It's the serious ones that sneak up on you without a word. And Matthew! He never tells me anything personal at all."

"Does he get home often? I imagine he's off in some scary part of the world."

"Yes. He's still working for Doctors Without Borders. He was back this spring for a visit. He never does talk about himself much, but, reading between the lines, I think he's ready to come home. I wouldn't be surprised to see him on my doorstep one day."

"Or Richard's?"

"Could be. I'd be happy with either." Their salads arrived just as Abby realized Summer had not made any comment on question two. She'd push it a little further after lunch. But she never did. Instead, over coffee, they took a trip down memory lane, recalling their college days.

"See," said Summer. "It was never me who led us into trouble."

"Nor I," said Abby. "We'll blame it all on Nikki."

"And she didn't live on campus, so she never had to face the consequences."

Abby shook her head at the waitress who arrived with a fresh coffee carafe. She was ready to float. She wanted to know if Summer had really been paying attention earlier, or just nodding, her head off somewhere else. "I'm really looking forward to having a reunion—all four of us. You were listening when we were talking about it?"

Summer looked affronted. "Of course I was. I think it's a grand idea. We'll do it as soon as your summer classes are over. What course are you teaching anyway? You never said."

"I'm teaching two. One is English for the Office and the other is Essay Writing. I was a little nervous about teaching again after all these years, but it's working out rather well. I don't see it on my long-term horizon, though. It's just a summer job to fill in the gaps until I get settled."

Summer reached for her handbag on the seat beside her. "Are you ready to go? Lunch is on me, by the way."

Abby protested, but Summer was adamant that it was her invitation, so she would pay. Abby settled for leaving the tip. She made it a generous one.

Summer pulled out of the parking lot, making a turn opposite the direction they'd arrived from.

Chapter
Ten

"Where are we going now? Isn't the ferry in the other direction?" Abby was a bit directionally challenged, but she was
positive they'd come in with the big Unicorn sign on their left.

"It's over an hour till the next one comes. We might as
well do some sight-seeing while we're here. There are some
cute little shops down the way and one in particular I want to
stop at. It's a little bakery that has fantastic herbal breads."

A few minutes later, she turned the car into a little com-
mercial area. It had several stores with boardwalk planking
and wooden overhangs giving it a crafty appearance, with
baskets of flowers hanging everywhere as well as in sidewalk
planters. Summer said, "We're probably interested in different things, so how about if you start at one end and I'll start
at the other. We'll meet at the car when we're done."

Abby browsed a used bookstore and was unable to leave
without buying a couple of books. She couldn't remember the
last time she'd left a bookstore—new or used—empty-handed.
She bypassed a vintage clothing shop. It depressed her to
think she was approaching an age when she might someday
remember wearing clothes featured there. Another shop sold
herbs, spices, and organic produce. By the time she left there,
she looked around to see where Summer had got to. She
spotted her coming out of the vintage shop she'd been in a

few minutes earlier. She was shoving something into the pocket of her purse. No purchases dangled from her arm.

A light came on for Abby. "You're not shopping!" she said. "You're sleuthing! That's the picture of Patsy you're try- ing to hide. You've been showing it around."

"Guilty. But it doesn't matter. No one has seen her, or at least doesn't remember. One lady said now that it's tourist season, she'd have to have walked in with two cobras draped over her arms for her to notice."

"Brrr," said Abby with a shiver. Snakes were another of her phobias, along with heights and closed spaces. She tried to banish the mental picture of Patsy with her slithery friends.

Back in the car, Summer said, "We might as well drive down to the end of the next road. I think there used to be an ice cream shop there. Maybe we can get some dessert. Then we can head for home."

They drove in silence until they came to a shack that looked as though it had seen better days. The windows were boarded over.

"I'm sure that's where the ice cream was," said Summer. "Or maybe it was down a bit. No, I'm sure this was it. Obvi- ously, it's closed."

"Looks like it's been closed for a while. When was the last time you were here?"

"A year or so ago. I'll make a u-turn here and we might as well head back to the ferry." Abby could hear the disap- pointment in her voice, but she didn't think it was for the nonexistent ice cream. She was sure it was Patsy on her mind.

She waited for a couple of vehicles to pass and then made a turn, veering on to the opposite shoulder. She stopped suddenly. "Look!"

"Where?"

"There! Right in front of your nose. That's Patsy." In her excitement, Summer had reverted to the name she was fa- miliar with. She pointed to a figure so shrouded Abby won- dered how she could recognize her. In spite of the warm day, the woman had a scarf over her head that covered most of her face. Her eyes were covered by large dark glasses. She wore jeans and an old shirt, probably a man's, as it was much too large for her.

Summer jumped out of the car and ran along the shoulder. Abby followed behind.

As she got close, Patsy came to a sudden halt, looking first at Summer, then around her as though seeking an escape.

"Patsy. I've been so worried about you. I'm glad to see you're safe. But what the heck is going on with you?"

Patsy continued to look this way and that and said, "I'm fine. You shouldn't bother with me. Look, I don't want to stand here talking."

"Then come in the car and we'll talk." She took her by the elbow, and Patsy, apparently seeing no alternative without creating a fuss, allowed herself to be pushed into the passenger seat. Abby relocated herself in the back.

"Where have you been staying?" Summer demanded.

"Down the road. I borrowed a little trailer from one of the girls I work with. It's parked over there in the campground."

"I think you mean 'worked with'," said Summer. "I called Ace Movers and they said you hadn't called in and I would very much doubt you have a job there anymore."

"No matter." Patsy shrugged.

"Why didn't your friend tell them where you were? It might have saved your job."

"I made her promise not to—to pretend she had no idea." She scrunched down in the seat of the car. "Can we move somewhere less visible?"

Summer complied and drove the car into a little side road.

"How is Peaches?"

"Fine, considering."

"Considering what?" Alarm showed on Patsy's face. "What happened to her?"

"Relax. Nothing happened to her. It's just that I never got your message till yesterday. My cell phone was broken and I just got it back and heard your message about looking after Peaches. Luckily, she got out somehow, maybe when you left, and came visiting. I took her home and fed her. She's fine."

The alarm returned to Patsy's face. "Peaches was indoors when I left," she said. "That means someone was in my house."

Abby gave Summer a warning glance, or tried to. It wasn't easy to catch her eye from the back seat. It was probably not a good idea to tell her they broke into her house before Summer got her message about Peaches. She thought back to the house as she remembered it. It didn't look as though intruders had been there. But then how could you tell in someone else's house what might be moved or missing?

Summer pressed Patsy for information. "Why did you come sneaking over to an out-of-the-way campground?"

"I didn't sneak. I left you a message, and anyhow, lots of people come here. The place is full. Why shouldn't I take a break?"

"Does this have anything to do with your brother getting out of jail?"

"How did you know about that?"

"Sorry. When Peaches came over and I didn't know where you were and I didn't have your message, I got worried. So Abby and I did a little sleuthing."

"Abby?" Patsy seemed to just now take note of the presence of a third party.

"Oh, I forgot to introduce you. This is Abby, an old college friend of mine. Abby—Patsy. Or should I say, Jenny."

"So how much do you know about me?"

"Only that your brother was in jail for killing his wife. Now I guess he's out. Is he the one you're afraid of?"

"Of course not! Douglas wouldn't hurt a fly, and he didn't kill Laura either." Abby realized she was telling the truth, about being frightened anyway. She'd been hiding as Patsy for years while her brother was in jail. It obviously wasn't him she was afraid of.

"Then who? And why go into hiding now?"

"It's really none of your business. But since you know part of it, you might as well know the rest." She sank down a little lower in the car seat, still looking uncomfortable. "It's a simple story, really. I married a jerk. Not just a jerk, but an abusive jerk. I left him after a couple of years, and I was so scared I ran away to stay with a cousin in another town. He followed me and made me come back with him."

"Made you? Couldn't you get a restraining order or something?" asked Summer.

Patsy snorted. "You know nothing about what men like

that can do. And nothing about how frightened they can make you. I went back with him. He promised to change. Sound familiar?" There was a hard edge of bitterness to her voice. "Then he started up again. To be sure I knew who was in charge, he had an affair with my sister-in-law, Douglas' wife Laura. He made sure I knew about it too. I finally decided I couldn't live like that anymore, but I planned it better this time. I managed to settle here under a different name with no relatives or friends he could track me to. And I've been safe. Then Laura got killed and Douglas got blamed and sent to jail and ..." She fished in her pocket for a tissue and blew her nose loudly, stuffing the tissue back.

"So Douglas is here and you go into hiding. But if not from him, then who? Did your ex-husband find out where you were living?"

"Not so far as I know. I haven't heard from him."

"Then who?"

"I can't tell you."

"Is your brother here at the campground with you?"

"Look, I know you want to help, but you can't. We have to figure this out for ourselves." She reached for the door handle. "Now I have to go. Don't tell anyone what you found out, please. Just pretend you never saw me." Then she stiffened as a car slowly drove by the lane they were parked in.

"Let me at least drop you off by the trailer," said Summer. "That way no one will see you walking in. Just scrunch down low and we'll drive into the park."

Patsy shut the door properly and turned her head towards the back of the car, pulling her scarf closer around her features.

Summer exited onto the road. The slow moving car had disappeared, so probably had just been looking for an address or maybe the campground. She pulled into the heavily treed grounds and followed Patsy's direction to their lot, near the far end. No vehicle was in the slot, so Summer pulled in and opened her door. Patsy climbed out and stood staring at the trailer. "The door is open," she whispered.

"Maybe your brother is there."

"No," said Patsy, turning. "I can't go in. He might be there." Abby wondered if she was still afraid of her ex, or if it was whoever Douglas was running from. Maybe they were one and the same.

"You wait in the car. We'll check." Summer motioned to Abby to join her and they cautiously approached the trailer.

Abby pulled the door open further and Summer was the first to enter. She turned back quickly without a word and ran to the bushes at the side of the lot. Abby could hear her retching. She knew she was about to witness something awful, but couldn't stop herself from crossing the trailer threshold. With a sudden horror, she saw what had sickened Summer. A man lay across the center of the trailer, head turned under the table, feet towards the rear bathroom. Blood pooled beside him and formed a swath where he had either moved or been dragged. There could be no doubt that the man was dead, not with that amount of blood. She couldn't see his face and wasn't about to try to move him.

She pulled back with a gasp and followed Summer. She could feel the bile rising in her throat and choked it down.

"There's a man in there and I'm sure he's dead. We have to call the police."

Chapter Eleven

Patsy scrambled out of the car seat and screamed, "Douglas!" running up the steps and inside before either Abby or Summer could stop her.

A moment later, she was back. "It's not Douglas," she said. "Thank heavens, it's Trevor." Abby noticed even then that she said it as one sentence, not two, and assumed the 'thank heavens' had as much to do with the fact that it was Trevor as that it wasn't Douglas.

Summer was already on her cell to the police. Luckily, the RCMP station wasn't far away. She could hear sirens almost immediately.

The three sat in the car waiting.

"So where is Douglas?" asked Summer. Abby bit her tongue to stop herself from saying he might have just been there and now was on the run.

"I don't know," said Patsy, tearing apart a moist tissue she held in her hand. "We were at the store picking up some supplies and he saw someone and took off. Told me to go home by myself."

"He's on foot?" asked Abby. If so, and he just left Patsy—er, Jenny—he wouldn't have had time to beat her to the trailer, kill the man inside, and disappear. Not unless he was a marathon runner.

Jenny looked as though she was going to agree. Then she shook her head. "No," she said, sniffling into her tissue. "He took the car."

"He has your car? But I thought..." How could she say someone saw them walking onto the ferry as foot passengers without losing what little connection they were making with her?

"It's not mine."

"Whose?" Summer barked out the question.

"It belongs to the same girl I'm renting the trailer from. It's an old beater and she leaves it on this side all summer. I'm paying her for it," she said defensively, misinterpreting their expressions. Both were thinking that gave Douglas more scope time wise. He could still have killed Trevor—just barely. Of course, they didn't know when he was killed. Either of them, or anyone else, could have done it earlier. Before the trip for supplies. Maybe the groceries they were going to get included clean up supplies. Abby noted Jenny's hands were empty. If they were shopping, where were the bags?

A police car pulled behind them. They could still hear sirens, so there must be an ambulance coming too, or maybe more police. A tall slim man with a ski slope nose, a receding hairline, and a toothbrush moustache appeared to be in command. He introduced himself, but Abby couldn't remember his name seconds later.

"Which of you found the body?" he asked after a quick foray into the trailer that must have assured him it was indeed a body.

"All of us," said Abby. At the same time, Summer was saying, "We were dropping Jenny off, and..." They were beginning to make the transformation of Patsy into Jenny.

The man in command turned to the passenger seat and said, "You're Jenny? Is this your trailer?"

"Yes," said Jenny quietly. "Or rather, it belongs to a friend and I'm renting it."

"Do you know who the man is inside? Did you get a look at him?"

"Yes. It's my ex-husband, Trevor."

His moustache quivered. Like a cat ready to pounce, thought Abby.

"Your ex-husband?" He gestured to another man in uniform and said, "This is Constable Perkins. He's going to escort all of you to the RCMP station. I'll need you to remain there until we're finished here. Then I'll need a statement from all of you."

"But my car is here," protested Summer.

"You can drive your car to the station. Constable Perkins will follow you with your friends." Abby wondered if they were being separated to be sure they didn't take off or to stop them from comparing notes before questioning.

He turned back to the trailer as the ambulance inched its way into the crowded parking spot.

Constable Perkins ushered Abby and Jenny into one of the police cars and steered around the other vehicles, out the lane to the road. Summer followed close behind in her car.

Perkins never spoke during the short ride to the police station. Abby also elected to keep quiet. Jenny stared out the window, scanning the edges of the road, as though looking for something. Or someone, corrected Abby. If that was Trevor in the trailer, where was Douglas? Jenny seemed genuinely not to know. Abby turned her head to look back, and Summer was following a few car lengths behind.

They were ushered into the station by the constable, and while Summer and Abby were left seated in the outer room in full view of the dispatch worker, Jenny was guided into a hallway. Abby lost sight of her, but whispered to Summer, "They don't want us to talk to her. They must think we'll work out a story."

"I wonder why they left us here?" asked Summer, then closed her mouth, quelled by a stern look from the woman in the dispatch booth.

"I guess Brunhilda here is supposed to keep us in line," Abby said, then giggled. She stopped quickly as she realized what an inappropriate reaction humor was to sudden death.

After that, they remained quiet, waiting.

It seemed forever, but according to the wall clock was less than an hour before the sergeant appeared. He motioned to them to follow him down the hall and sent Summer into a small interview room, leaving Abby on a lone chair in the hallway. She could hear a murmur of voices coming from another room behind her and knew that must be someone taking a statement from Jenny.

Soon, Summer came out of the room, followed by her interviewer, who now motioned Abby to come in.

He flicked a switch, a recorder of some sort, and announced his name, the date, and Abby's name. She wondered how he knew her full name, but guessed Summer had told him. She tried to remember his name now that she'd heard it again. Weaver! Why did she have trouble with such a simple name? Maybe she should use a mnemonic memory aid. She'd picture him seated at a loom. She started and came out of her reverie as he began the questions.

The questions were terse and easily answered. She suspected Summer had done the heavy lifting question-wise and she was merely confirming what they already knew.

"Why were you there in the first place?" he asked. "Had you ever met Jenny Donaldson before?"

So, obviously, Jenny had told them her real name, but then she had no choice. They had already called her that.

"No," answered Abby. "She's the neighbor of my friend, Summer. Summer was looking after her cat while she was camping. We ran into her by accident today."

The sergeant gave her a skeptical look.

"We did. We came over for lunch at the Unicorn and then went for a drive because we had an hour or so to kill before the next ferry. Oh dear, we've missed it now, haven't we?"

"There will be more ferries," said Sergeant Weaver.

"Anyway," Abby continued. "We were driving around and were going to get some ice cream, only the place is closed, and then we saw Jenny, walking down the road, and Summer recognized her, so we stopped to talk. Then we gave her a ride home."

"Why did you go into the trailer?"

"Jenny saw the door was open, so we thought we should stay with her until we knew no one had broken in. Summer looked in first, then me and then Jenny. When we said someone was in there dead, Jenny was afraid it was her brother, Douglas."

Abby could feel herself babbling. She should answer only what she was asked, she knew, not embellish. A police station was such an intimidating place. It made you feel as though you had no secrets, so you might as well just talk.

But she didn't have secrets, at least not her own. And it looked as though any secrets Jenny had weren't secrets any longer.

"Did you recognize the man? How did you know it wasn't Douglas Martindale?"

"I didn't. I've never met Douglas. An hour ago, I'd never met Jenny either. Besides, he was turned so I couldn't see the face. I could tell he was dead and just ran out of there. Then Jenny came in and said it wasn't Douglas; it was her ex, Trevor."

"How did you know he was dead? Did you check for a pulse?"

"No, I could tell he was dead because of all the blood and he wasn't moving."

"So you never touched the body?"

Abby didn't need to think. She had bolted when she had seen him. "No."

"How did Jenny react when she saw the body?"

"I wasn't really paying attention. She was relieved, of course, that it wasn't her brother, but she was just as shocked as we were that someone was dead in her trailer."

"Hmmm." said Sergeant Weaver. "That's all I need from you now. We need to get a printed and signed statement from you and then you can go. Be sure to leave your address and phone numbers."

"Can we take Jenny with us?'"

"I'll let you know shortly. She's still being interviewed. You can wait out front."

By the time Abby had signed her statement, Summer was pacing the entry room, stopping to peer out the door at every turn around the room.

"There you are!" she nearly shouted when Abby joined her. They both sat down in chairs as far away from the listening ears of the dispatch officer as they could.

"What did you tell them?" Summer demanded.

"Not much. I don't know much to tell. I just answered the questions they asked."

"Did you tell them about our research?"

"No. They didn't ask. I don't imagine they'd care. Anything we found out will be old news to them. I imagine they talked to the police station where you reported Jenny missing."

"What should we do now?"

"Sergeant Weaver said they were still talking to Jenny, and if we waited they'd let us know if we could take her home."

"I wish they'd hurry." Summer took a quick glance at her watch. "There's only one more ferry today and I don't fancy paying to stay at a hotel here."

"Me neither," said Abby. "But since Jenny can't go back to the trailer, she either has to come with us or..."

"Or be arrested," finished Summer.

"I don't imagine they know enough yet to take that kind of action."

"You never know. That sergeant looked pretty single-minded to me. If he gets an idea in his head, I bet it would take dynamite to get it out."

"I don't think the police act like that," said Abby. "They have to have a good reason and evidence to arrest someone." She knew Summer wasn't a great fan of the police. Back in her younger days, she'd been involved in a few protests that ended in altercations with law enforcement. But this wasn't chaining yourself to a tree to stop loggers. This was murder.

Eventually, after a half hour of sporadic bursts of conversation, punctuated by Summer's staring at her watch, apparently willing it to stop, a police constable ushered Jenny to the front.

Abby and Summer both jumped up.

"Are you coming with us?"

Jenny looked around and said, "They told me I was free to go home, just not to leave town. But I don't want to leave the island. I need to find Douglas."

"The police will find Douglas, I'm sure. They'll need to talk to him."

"I want to talk to him first," said Jenny.

"Why?" asked Abby.

"Never mind. It doesn't matter." But Abby could see that it did.

"We have to get going," said Summer. "The ferry leaves in ten minutes."

"You go ahead," said Jenny.

"No!" said Summer and Abby together. Summer went on. "You can't stay here. The trailer is off limits. Staying in a hotel won't help you find Douglas. He wouldn't know where to find you. Your best hope is to go back home and hope he looks for you there."

Jenny thought a moment and reluctantly agreed. Heaving a sigh of relief, Summer ushered them all to the parking lot and then into her car. She swirled out of the lot and took them on a quick and scary drive to the ferry. They almost missed it. As soon as they drove on, the ferry began its slow trek across the passage.

When they drove off at the other end, Summer said, "I'll drop you off first, Abby, and then I'll get Jenny back home."

In spite of her insistence on going home, Jenny looked a little apprehensive at the thought. Then Abby remembered the escaped Peaches and wondered if Jenny had told the RCMP about her possible intruder.

"Maybe Jenny would feel safer at my house," she said.

"No. I want to be home in case Douglas calls."

Abby's stomach did a slow rumble. Had it really been that long since the huge lunch they had? She looked at her watch and realized it was. "Would anyone like to stop for a quick burger somewhere first?" she asked. She pushed back her guilt about insensitivity in the face of death. Hunger was a physical need. You had to eat.

"No," said Jenny quickly. "I'm sure there will be something in the fridge that hasn't gone bad. I'll make do."

"Then let's at least do a drive-through."

Jenny nodded. "Okay, a burger and fries would work for me. As long as it's to go."

Summer dropped Abby off with the bag of aromatic fast food that had called to her empty stomach all the way home. Then she drove off with Jenny.

Chapter Twelve

Ajax was at her feet the minute she walked in the door. He could smell the burger too. She filled his cat dish, but knew he would ignore it until her food was out of the way.

She grabbed a plate from the cupboard and unloaded her meal onto it. Then she took a partial bottle of white wine from the fridge and poured a liberal glass to go with it. She took her meal into the living room and turned on the television. Her shoulders were knotted with tension and she hoped to find something to relax her. She flicked the remote and all she could find were documentaries and reality shows and old sit-coms she'd never watched for the first go-round. Finally, she decided to watch one of the reality shows where the contestants competed to lose weight. Just what she needed with a plateful of grease staring at her.

Ajax circled Abby's seat and, not getting the attention or food he felt he deserved, climbed onto the arm of the chair, batting at Abby's arm. She relented and offered him a small piece of burger. She knew it was a bad thing to do. Once offered food from a plate, he'd expect it all the time now. Then she realized he expected it all the time anyhow, so she gave him another bite.

She wondered if Summer had stayed with Jenny to eat or if she checked her house first. Then she thought about the note from Blanche. They never had told Jenny about that. Summer never said what she did with it after reading it to Abby on the phone. Did she put it back in the mail box?

The phone rang. It was in Abby's purse in the kitchen. She jumped up to find it and, on second thought, grabbed her plate to bring with her. Nothing would be left but pickle and crumbs if she left it unattended.

She took a quick look at the display before answering. She half expected Neil might follow up on his unanswered e-mails. She wasn't sure if she was relieved or disappointed to see it was Summer. What had happened now?

Summer's voice was unusually quiet.

"Why are you whispering?"

"I'm at Jenny's. She's asleep upstairs. At least, I hope she's asleep."

"She decided she needed company after all. That's good."

"It wasn't for the company. I came in with her to see if everything was all right. She looked around and said she was sure someone had been in her house."

"They were. We were," said Abby. She tried to remember what they might have disturbed when they were looking for answers to Jenny's disappearance. Abby had turned on her computer, but put it back exactly where it was. The only other things they had disturbed were her uniform shirt in the closet and the newspaper on the bedside table.

"No, this was different. She said someone had been looking through her papers. She had some old letters in a drawer in the kitchen and they were scattered around in different order than she'd left them. Jenny is super neat, so I think she's probably right about someone being in there."

"It wasn't us, was it? We never went into her private letters. We never found any."

"No." Summer's answer was quick and definite.

"Did you tell her about our looking around?"

"Yes. She seemed a little annoyed we were checking on her, but finally seemed to realize we were worried about her, not snooping."

"Well, worried and snooping," corrected Abby. "But I'm glad she knows. Wait!" Abby remembered the note from Blanche. "Did you give her the note?"

"She found it. After I read it to you, I put it back in the

box. I didn't bother telling her we'd read it. She was already upset about our looking around."

"So, who does she think was in her house? And how did they get in?"

"She wouldn't say. It can't be Trevor she's worried about because he's dead. She must be worried about someone else."

"I'm glad she let you stay with her. But be careful. If someone was there before, they could come back. Unless it was Trevor. He certainly won't be coming back."

"Thanks for the reassurance, Abby. I'll sleep much better now."

Abby mentally kicked herself for raising her fears. "Sorry. It would have been much better if Jenny had gone to your place instead."

"I tried, but she wouldn't budge. She's afraid she'll miss a call from Douglas."

"Doesn't she have a cell phone? She could take it with her. Why would he call on her land line?" Abby never went twenty feet without taking her cell. She assumed everyone else did the same.

"She doesn't have a cell. Don't ask me why because I don't know."

"If he's in hiding, he likely won't come to her house. He'd be afraid the police would be watching for him. Same goes for phone calls. Maybe they're monitoring her phone."

"I think they need a warrant or something for that." Summer's voice was still a loud whisper.

Abby waited for a comment about police not always operating by the book, but it didn't follow. Maybe Summer's views on law enforcement had mellowed now that she no longer tied herself to trees. "I imagine they do," said Abby. "Do you think she'll tell the police about someone breaking in?"

"I mentioned it. She said they wouldn't pay much attention if all she had to tell them was an old letter or two being moved. No one broke the door lock. They must have found an easier way in." Abby could almost hear the shudder over the phone.

"Well, keep your cell beside you."

"I will. And a hammer for good measure." Summer gave a nervous giggle.

"Oh, I forgot to ask. Did she say what the letters were that were disturbed? No one writes letters much these days. Were they old?"

"Apparently, they were letters from Douglas when he was in prison."

"So, what would they be looking for in those letters?" Then Abby had a thought. "Do you think it's Douglas someone is after, and not Jenny?"

"Could very well be. I hope the police find him soon."

"But if he killed Trevor, it's going to be hard on Jenny."

"She's convinced he didn't kill Trevor. She's so adamant, she has me believing her."

"The police might be a little more difficult to convince," said Abby.

"Don't you think it's strange," said Summer, "that the police seem to be more focused on Douglas than they are on Jenny? After all, it was her ex-husband who's dead."

"Well, Douglas is an ex-con. He's killed once. Then, too, maybe it's because he's disappeared. That's not usually a good sign."

"But did he? Maybe he was off somewhere else and didn't even know Trevor was dead or at the trailer. He's only staying away because he saw someone he's worried about? Jenny never said exactly who or what it was that spooked Douglas in the store."

"He should know by now, though. And he's still AWOL."

"I guess you're right." Summer's agreement sounded reluctant and unconvincing.

"Then, too, maybe Trevor wasn't dead very long," said Abby. "The police must have a general idea. And Jenny was with us before we found him and before that in the store and walking home. There would be witnesses to the store excursion. When would she have killed him? And when would she have cleaned herself up?"

"I'm going to try to go to sleep now. I'll talk to you in the morning." Summer was still whispering. Abby could picture her on the couch with one eye turned to the stairway watching for Jenny. If her eyes weren't riveted on the front door waiting for a doorknob to turn. Darn! It would have been better if she had gone with them instead of being dropped at home. Then there would be two of them to watch the front door. And two hammers by the bedside. Too late now, though. She couldn't really invite herself into a sleeping woman's house.

"I have one early class, then nothing more until a night course. I'll be home elevenish. Give me a call then. Or leave a message on my phone if anything new happens and I'll get to you when I can."

Abby threw the remains of her supper in the trash after picking out the meaty morsels for Ajax. He took the offering as no more than his due. Cold French fries were not an appetizing sight. And they tasted even worse heated up.

She checked her e-mails. Nothing other than junk or promos of some sort. She knew sooner or later she was going to have to answer Neil, but right now she wanted it to be later. It seemed as though the past day had had forty-eight hours in it instead of twenty-four.

She brushed, flossed, and pulled on a short nightgown, ready for bed. She looked around for something to read and selected an old novel to take to bed with her. She didn't feel at all sleepy and the familiar words of a once-read book could lull her off to dreamland.

Her iPad was on the side table and, before she shut it down, it gave a ping announcing new mail. She knew it would likely be trash, but curiosity wouldn't help her sleep so she checked it.

It was from Mandy. *"Mom, I just heard on the news there was a suspicious death on Quadra. Please tell me this has nothing to do with you. Your last text said you were over there with Summer for lunch."*

Abby reached for the pad to answer, but decided to phone instead. The e-mail had just arrived, so obviously, Mandy was awake.

She answered on the first ring.

"Hi, Mom. I hope you're keeping out of trouble." The words were lighthearted but Abby could sense the concern behind them.

"I'm the mother here. That's what I'm supposed to be saying to you."

"But you're the one who has the annoying habit of getting involved in other people's problems. Is everything all right? Did you know whoever was killed?"

"I don't understand how you heard about it. It just happened a while ago. It's on the news already?"

"So you do know all about it."

Abby sighed. "There was a death. I didn't know the person who died, but I have met his ex-wife. She lives next door to Summer."

"Every time you meet up with old college friends, it gets you into trouble. First it was Nikki, now it's Summer. I think you better put off that visit to Jessica."

"This isn't the same, dear. I am not involved in this. Well, except for finding the body, of course."

"You found the body?" Mandy's voice was rising, either in alarm or excitement.

Abby gave her daughter the brief story about their day on Quadra. She had already told her about the missing Patsy/Jenny. Now she filled in the gaps about Jenny's past life and how they had found first her, and then Trevor. So you see," she finished, "it wasn't me doing the snooping today. It was Summer. But now the police are involved and the rest is up to them. Summer and I are well and truly out of it."

"Maybe I should come out for a few days and stay with you."

"You can't," protested Abby. "You can't take time off from your classes. And, anyhow, as I said, it has nothing more to do with us. We gave a statement and now the police are looking for Jenny's brother."

After a brief silence at the other end of the line, Abby said, "You haven't been talking to your father tonight, have you?"

"Well, I talked to him just now and told him the little bit I knew. He's worried about you too."

"And he put you up to checking on me?"

"Something like that."

"Well, you can both relax. I'm sure they'll have Douglas found and arrested by tomorrow and it will be all over. If he did it, that is."

"Mom!" The warning tone was stronger now.

"His sister is so positive he didn't do it."

"Of course. She's his sister. What else would she say?'

"She has Summer convinced there's more to it. But you're right. Prisons are full of guilty people protesting their innocence. But we know the odd one is telling the truth." Her sentence began confidently, but trailed off in uncertainty. "No, you're right," she said again. "It's not up to me. I have a job now to look after with a class first thing in the morning. I'm going to concentrate on that and get some sleep."

"Okay. Good night, Mom. Keep out of trouble."

"Goodnight, love. And Mandy?"

"Yes."

"Thanks for worrying, even if it's not necessary."

She lay back against her stacked pillows, even less ready for sleep now. She thought about the letters in Jenny's drawer that were disturbed. What interest could they have for anyone? And who was Douglas running from? If it was Trevor, then his problems were over, unless, that is, he was arrested for the murder, which was beginning to seem likely.

She couldn't think of any reason Trevor would be rummaging in Jenny's mail. If he had been stalking or looking for Jenny, he had already found her. If he was looking for Douglas, why not confront him when he was in prison, or go to his home when he got out? Then she remembered the note from Blanche. But why would Douglas be hiding from his mother-in-law? The same arguments applied to her. She knew where he was all along. That led her back to the man in denim. Maybe he was looking for something and only left when he thought he was being watched. He could have come back later.

Somehow, Jenny was the common factor here even if she didn't seem to have the opportunity to kill Trevor. Douglas hadn't been in hiding. Jenny had.

Everyone had converged at her home—Douglas, Trevor, Blanche, Denim Man. Had the other three followed Douglas? Possibly four, if none of the others were responsible. Douglas wouldn't root in her drawers, Trevor had no reason to, and Blanche appeared to take the direct route, leaving a message openly for Jenny. That left X. Who could X be? Denim Man seemed the best bet, only because he was the unknown.

She turned off her iPad and shut the sound off on her phone so she wouldn't be awakened to check her e-mail. Then she set the phone on vibrate and tucked it under her pillow. That way she'd be aware of a call coming in but could ignore other posts and mail.

She expected to lie awake with her mind in such a muddle, but strangely, sleep came quickly, also dreamlessly.

Chapter
Thirteen

When Abby awoke, the sun was streaming through her bedroom window and Ajax was sitting on the other pillow, staring at her through blinking eyes. At least he wasn't mauling her head as he did some mornings.

She looked after his needs, had a quick shower and a quicker breakfast. In spite of her long dreamless sleep, she felt tired and dozy this morning.

Abby labored through her early class, having to force her concentration. Unfortunately, her annoying questioner was absent. He might have kept the conversation going a little more speedily.

As soon as she had finished her class, she turned on her cell, expecting messages from Summer. Nothing. She stopped at a drive-through for a coffee, deciding against the doughnut, but surely a scone was a healthy alternative, even covered with butter. What was worse for you, fat or sugar?

She took her coffee and scone home with her. When she had finished the scone, she sat and stared at the silent phone. *It's none of your business, Abby*, she repeated to herself. *The police are in charge now*. Still, it was annoying that Summer hadn't at least left a message. But then, of course, if she was still with Jenny, she couldn't talk anyway.

She dialed Summer's cell. It rang busy. She waited a few

minutes and dialed again. Still busy. She finally gave up. She wasn't going to accomplish anything till she found out what she was missing.

She threw the remains of her coffee down the drain and grabbed her purse and keys. Time to beard the lion in his, or rather her, den.

Summer answered the door at her first knock as though she'd been watching her pull up. "I've been trying to call you," she said accusingly.

"That's why your phone kept ringing busy. I thought maybe you were talking to Jennifer."

"No, I'm trying to avoid her till this gets settled. She'll know by my voice something is up, and I'm no good at lying to her. Then she'll be upset and worried."

"Tell me about it. Mandy saw the news and called last night. She thinks I'm getting involved in something again."

"Well, it was Mandy that dragged you into it last year, after all." Summer dismissed her concern. "I don't think this will make the news in Massachusetts, so hopefully, I won't have to tell Jennifer the story till it's all over." They were still standing in the foyer. Summer said, "You'd better come in," and led the way to the living room. They took seats opposite each other in front of the fireplace. Summer had a low flame going. "It was cool this morning," she said. "Do you want tea?" She reached over to shut the gas flame off.

"No thanks. I finished a double-double of coffee. I just want to hear more about last night."

"There's nothing more to tell you. Jenny went up to bed almost as soon as we got in. She picked up the phone a few times first to be sure she had a dial tone. Then she gave me some blankets and opened the hide-a-bed."

"I was going to ask—why did she put you on the couch? Doesn't she have two bedrooms?"

"Apparently one is full of Douglas' things, so I got the couch."

"Not exactly Ms. Hospitality, is she?" Then she thought — *or maybe she wanted you downstairs to be the first in the line of fire.* Happily, she didn't verbalize the sentiment.

"No, but, after all she's been through—an abusive husband, a brother in jail and now missing, finding her ex murdered—I think we can cut her a little slack."

Abby agreed shame-facedly. Where had her empathy flown? "You're right. I was being annoyed at her secretiveness, and that's silly, isn't it? It's her life, and if she doesn't want outsiders in, that's her business."

"Agreed. Now we leave it up to the police. It's their job after all." They both sat back at that conclusion with matching gloomy faces. Abby began to giggle and soon Summer was joining in.

"I'm going to make some tea, anyhow," said Summer. "You may not need it, but I do."

She headed for the kitchen, but as she passed the hallway leading to the front door, she stopped and stiffened.

"What is it?" asked Abby.

"A car just pulled up at Jenny's. Do you think it could be Douglas?"

Abby leapt up to join her as they watched the visitor exit the car. "Not Douglas—a woman!" said Abby.

"Blanche," added Summer.

They pulled back from line of sight into Summer's foyer. "We said we weren't going to get involved again," said Abby. "I think I will join you in that up of tea."

They returned to the living room and made desultory conversation, neither of them sipping at the teacups in front of them, both with their minds on next door. As one, they sat up quickly with startled expressions as the knocker sounded loudly on Summer's door.

Abby ushered Blanche in from the front step. "I'm sorry to bother you," she said. "But I'm trying to contact your neighbor and she doesn't appear to be home. I left a message before, but I don't know if she got it. Could I leave one with you?"

"You're Blanche, Douglas's mother-in-law." Unfazed by Blanche's double-take, she went on." I'm Summer, and this is my friend Abby. We're both in Jenny's confidence, so feel free to tell us anything you want to pass on to her."

Summer led Blanche into the living room and pressed a cup of tea onto her.

"Well, since you seem to know all about it," she began, a doubtful note in her voice.

"We do know about your daughter Laura." Summer reached over to give Blanche's hand a squeeze. "We're so sorry. We also know Douglas was convicted and just got out of jail. He seems to be missing at the moment, so maybe Jenny hasn't had a chance to give him the note." Abby was about to interject that they knew very well she had lots of opportunity to tell him, but Summer gave her a quelling look and Abby bit the inside of her cheek to will herself silent. She'd let Summer take the lead. It was her house and her guest, after all.

Blanche let out a long breath. "I've hated Douglas with a passion for the past four years," she began slowly. "He took away the best part of my life—Laura was a lovely person, warm and sunny, honest and just plain good, something you don't often see nowadays." Her eyes misted over and she reached down to fumble in her purse for a tissue. Abby and Summer exchanged glances over her head. They were about to finally get the true story. Blanche sniffled and went on. "At least, that's what I thought. Then I received a letter from Laura."

"A letter? But How?" were the simultaneous responses.

"Apparently, it had been lost in the mail somehow. I don't know. I only know it was written by my daughter a few days before she was killed."

"You're certain it was from her?"

"I think I know my own daughter's handwriting." Blanche seemed affronted by the question. Abby was thinking, *How unusual in this day and age—an actual handwritten letter.*

"She told me in the letter how frightened she was—not of Douglas, but of Trevor, Jenny's ex. Apparently, he had been trying to start a relationship with her and was becoming increasingly threatening when she wouldn't agree. She was telling me in this letter if anything happened to her, I should tell the police to look for Trevor. It was him who killed my Jenny, not Douglas. And that means I owe him not only an apology for not believing him, but I also owe him the truth. He needs to clear his name."

Abby tried to sort the new information as Blanche talked. Which version was correct—Jenny's story that Trevor and Laura were having an affair, or Laura's insistence that they weren't? It didn't really matter. It all came down to the same thing in the end. Trevor had a motive. He might not have planned to kill Laura, but he probably was trying to bully her into something and the violence got out of hand. Poor Doug-las! Four years in jail for a crime he didn't commit. Or at least that's the way it appeared. There was no more evi-dence against Trevor than there was against Douglas. Except for Laura. She must have felt in fear of her life. Why in the world didn't she confide in her husband? Unless there really was an affair—or she feared he would think there was one.

"Do you want us to give the letter to Douglas when he comes back? Or pass it on to Jenny when we see her?"

Blanche looked a little embarrassed. "Well, I'd love to pass it on. But I seem to have misplaced it somewhere. But I do want to let him know what it said. Would it be all right if I wrote it out as best I can remember?"

"Of course," said Summer.

Abby realized with a start that Blanche might not have heard the news. Did she know Trevor had been killed?

She locked her gaze onto Summer's over Blanche's bent head as she scribbled down a facsimile of the letter. They waited a moment as she wrote. Then Abby nodded to indi-cate the news should come from Summer.

"Uh, Blanche..." Summer began. "There's something you might not know." She went on to describe meeting Jenny on Quadra and finding Trevor dead in the trailer.

Blanche's head jerked up. "Dead? You mean actually dead? Not just injured?"

It seemed a strange reaction, but Abby and Summer both nodded.

"But I was sure..." Blanche's forehead tightened into a frown as she digested the news. Then she jumped up sud-denly and said, "I have to go. I shouldn't have come. I'm sorry."

She grabbed her purse and keys and stumbled to the front door without another word. Abby and Summer stood to follow, but she was out the door like a startled animal run-ning from a gunshot.

"Well!" said Abby, collapsing on the couch from her standing position. "That takes the cake."

"It seems strange that she's so shook up over the death of the man who probably killed her daughter," Summer agreed.

"There's more to it than that, I'm sure," said Abby. Then

her glance fell to the handwritten note on the coffee table. "At least she left the letter—the copy of it, that is."

Summer sighed. "I guess we'd better go next door and tell Jenny." She picked up the letter and said, "Let's go."

"But Jenny won't answer the door. Blanche knocked and knocked."

"That's because she didn't want to talk to Blanche. She'll talk to us." She nodded grimly. "We'll keep knocking and calling until she opens up. Jenny doesn't want to alert the neighbors to what's going on, so she'll let us in to avoid a scene."

They made their way to Jenny's front door and, surprisingly, it opened on the first knock. Jenny had probably been watching from behind the window.

She opened the door to let them in, but stood in the hallway, stony-eyed and arms crossed, as though guarding an inner sanctum. "I saw Blanche go into your place," she said. "What story was she telling you?"

"A good one, from Douglas' point of view," said Summer. "I think you'll want to hear it."

At that, Jenny stopped and stiffened. Then her shoulders relaxed and she seemed to thaw. She led them into the kitchen, gesturing at the chairs arranged around the kitchen table. They slid into seats side by side at the back of the table, facing Jenny, waiting for her to join them.

"Coffee?" she asked. "This is stale, but I can make some fresh."

"No thanks," they both echoed.

Jenny sat down across the table from them. "We could use some good news," she said. "What is it?"

Summer pulled the copied letter from her pocket and handed it to Jenny. "Blanche says she received this from Laura, but for some reason, it didn't arrive until five years later. She just got it a few days ago."

"It must be the one Douglas mailed to her."

"Pardon?" Both Summer and Abby were thinking the same thought. Blanche said she recognized her daughter's handwriting, but was there some way Douglas could have counterfeited the letter?

"Oh, it was from Laura all right," said Jenny. "Douglas found it in an old purse of hers when he was looking for something else. It was all stamped and ready to mail, but for some reason, she never sent it. Douglas threw it in a letter box without opening it. Silly thing to do. I told him so. There might have been something in it to help him prove his innocence."

"Apparently there was," said Abby. But Jenny was already reading.

"This is wonderful!" said Jenny. "It shows Trevor had more motive to kill Laura than Douglas had. And it shows she was frightened of him. Why oh why didn't she talk to Douglas about it? Why write to her mother? Why not phone her?" Then Jenny stopped and gave the letter another glance. "Wait a minute," she said. "It's not even signed. It's not finished either. It just trails off. And I know Laura's handwriting; this isn't it." She looked up at them and suddenly stopped, apparently becoming aware that she was undercutting all the possibilities the letter held for exonerating her brother.

"It's all right," soothed Abby. "It's not the original. It's Blanche's handwriting. She misplaced the original somewhere and copied it out the best she could remember for us."

"Thank heavens!" said Jenny. "But we need that original to take to the police. Oh why doesn't Douglas call me? Now he has nothing to be afraid about."

Maybe nothing about the old murder, but it's the new one the police are looking to question him for.

Jenny apparently had the same thought. "I'm sure the police will figure out who killed Trevor," she said. "And it wasn't Douglas. It will help them make up their minds when they realize he was falsely imprisoned for killing Laura. That's the only thing against him here."

Not really, thought Abby. *He hates Trevor for what he did to you and he would hate him more if he realized Trevor killed Laura.*

"Did Blanche give you a phone number?" asked Jenny. "I have to call her. I have to get that original."

Abby bit her lip to stop from saying she knew Blanche's number was on her note to Douglas. Instead, she framed it as a question. "Didn't you say Blanche left a note in your mailbox?" When Jenny nodded, she went on, "Maybe she left a number there for Douglas to call her?"

"She did, but I don't have that note. Douglas does."

"Well, I'm sure we can track her down somehow. There's no sense looking her up in the white pages. It will only list her land line, but as soon as Douglas calls..."

The phone rang then as if on cue. All three of them jumped and Jenny threw herself at the phone.

"Hello? Douglas? Is it really you? Thanks heavens. You'll never guess what happened..."They watched as her expression changed from delight to apprehension to shock. "No, you can't be serious."

Jenny turned from Abby and Summer and wandered, phone in hand, out of the room. Abby's eyes met Summer's. Douglas might have turned up, but it didn't sound good.

Chapter Fourteen

Jenny disappeared from sight, but they could hear the low murmur of her voice. Then it stopped and they waited for her to return to the kitchen. When she didn't reappear, they exchanged nervous smiles as they wondered what to do. Follow her into the living room or wait for her to come back? It seemed as though she had forgotten their presence.

"You have to go!" Jenny suddenly stood framed in the kitchen doorway, still holding her phone.

They stood as one, scraping chairs along the tile floor.

"What's happened? Is Douglas all right?"

"They've arrested him, the idiots! He's in jail and I have to go see him."

"Shouldn't you call a lawyer first?"

Jenny swiped a distracted hand through her hair, pushing it back from her face. "Yes, you're right. I'll call someone. Who?"

Abby had no idea to give her; she was a newcomer. Summer shrugged and said, "I'm afraid I don't know any attorneys. At least not here. Let's get the yellow pages and have a look." She took Jenny by the arm and led her back to the table. "Where's your phone book?"

Jenny pointed to a drawer at the end of the cupboards and sat wordlessly as Summer picked a name at random—

one with a fair-sized ad, which should indicate a healthy business.

She dialed the number and put the phone in Jenny's hand. Jenny gave it a startled look as though wondering how it came to be there and sprang into life at the sound of an answering voice. Again, she detoured into the other room to carry on her conversation.

In a few minutes, she was back. "Someone is going over to see Douglas and decide if they can help him. Now," she said, looking around. "You have to go. I must get over there and make sure they know he's innocent. I'll show them the letter Blanche left. I wish I had the original, but this will have to do."

She stared at them as if wondering why they were still there. They took their cue and stood to leave.

"Wait," said Summer. "Do you have a car? You left your friend's car on Quadra."

"Douglas had that. I still have my car here. I didn't take it because I didn't want... Never mind. I have to go."

Jenny picked up keys from the countertop, along with her purse, and shooed them out the door in front of her.

Back in Summer's living room, Abby sat limply on the couch and looked across at Summer, who wore the same attitude of bewilderment she felt.

"So," she began, "if they have Douglas in custody, they must have him pegged for Trevor's murder."

"But we know he didn't kill Laura. So why Trevor?"

"We don't know for a fact Douglas didn't kill his wife. We only know someone else could have—that Laura was frightened of Trevor. As far as I can see, it's a wash as to which one of them did it."

"Jenny seems so sure..."

"Well, she would. She's his sister. And she has plenty of reason to hate Trevor."

"But Blanche was pretty certain, too, that Trevor did it."

"I think Jenny has you brainwashed into thinking Douglas is innocent. She keeps insisting over and over and, eventually, it just seems to be true."

"I'm not brainwashed," said Summer crossly. "But Douglas, Jenny, and Blanche all had reason to hate Trevor. And who is this mystery man that's been hanging around?"

"Oh, I forgot about him." Abby stopped to think. "It can't be Jenny who killed him. We picked her up just before we found him. She was on foot and coming from the other direction. And she had no blood or anything on her."

"Maybe she slipped off somewhere and cleaned up," said Summer. Then she revised that thought. "No, I think Trevor must have been killed shortly before we got there. That's why the police didn't keep Jenny after we were all questioned. She wouldn't have been able to kill him, clean up, then sit and talk to us for a half hour or so. We're her alibi."

"Okay, scratch Jenny from the list. There's always Blanche. She just found out that Trevor, in all likelihood, killed her daughter after she spent five years thinking it was her son-in-law."

"But then why would she be so anxious to exonerate Douglas? If she kept quiet, no one would know about Trevor and Laura. They would latch on to Douglas as the likeliest suspect for killing Trevor because he already committed one murder."

"Conscience?" asked Abby.

"Do murderers have that much conscience?"

"But if she didn't kill Trevor?"

"You can't have it both ways, Abby. Either she's a murderer who wants to cover her tracks, or she's innocent and trying to right a wrong."

Abby sighed. "I suppose you're right. But I'm sure a killer might want to get away and still not want to see the wrong person accused. No, I don't think we can write off Blanche."

"And Denim Man?" asked Summer.

"What was he after? Is he the one who was looking through Douglas's old letters? Is that when Peaches made her escape? Or was he someone from Jenny's job trying to find out what happened to her?"

Summer considered a moment. "I don't think he was from work. The company didn't appear concerned enough about her absence to send someone looking for her. They would simply get along without her and hire someone else."

"Maybe. Then who was he?"

Chapter Fifteen

Next morning, Abby woke with the delicious thought that today she had no classes. Yesterday's evening class had gone by in a blur of semi-consciousness. She wondered if her students had noticed her distraction. If they did, they had made no mention. Today, Abby needed a chance to clarify her thoughts.

When the conversations of yesterday surfaced, she fought to sort out the events. She wondered if Jenny had been able to talk to Douglas. Maybe not if he was still being questioned. She hoped the lawyer would help get the information to the attention of the police. Then she stopped and rethought that. Maybe it didn't need sorting out. Maybe Douglas was the murderer after all. Was she "brainwashed" into believing his innocence as well? Jenny was a convincing advocate for her brother.

At that point, Ajax decided Abby had been awake long enough to be moving to the kitchen to take care of his breakfast. He bounced on the bed and sat on the pillow next to her head. She knew a lie-in was a lost cause, so she reluctantly threw off her comforter and slipped into her robe before Ajax had a chance to get orange tabby claws tangled in her hair.

Showered and dressed, she stood in front of an open fridge door, sipping coffee and scanning the contents. Comfort or health food? She picked up the carton of eggs and decided she could have it both ways. A simple omelette with chopped peppers and no cheese would be the both of best worlds. She'd cut back the toast to one slice. She wasn't sure she believed all that "wheat belly" stuff, but bread was a weakness of hers so maybe there was something in it. She cast a rueful downward glance at her not so svelte tummy and sighed. Neil always told her—no, she wasn't going to even think about Neil.

She was nearly finished with her omelette when the phone rang. A glance at the display showed it was Summer. Maybe there was news. She swallowed her last bite too quickly and began a paroxysm of coughing as she pressed the answer button.

By the time she recovered, Summer was nearly yelling into the phone. "Abby, are you all right?"

She managed to convince her she was fine, took a gulp of coffee to get rid of the last remnants of crumb in her throat, and said in a raspy voice, "What's up?"

"Blanche is up, that's what."

"What do you mean?"

"She's back at Jenny's door. She's not answering, and I'm sure she'll do like last time. She'll come over here. Get over here quickly and you can help me explain to her about Douglas being arrested." She hung up.

Abby wasn't sure why Summer couldn't explain to Blanche herself, but as always, her curiosity bug slipped into high gear. She threw her breakfast dishes in the sink, grabbed her keys and purse, and dashed out to her car, headed for Summer's condo. In five minutes, she was pulling into the visitor slot. Good thing she didn't live on the far side of town; the action would be over before she got there. Maybe it would anyhow.

She knocked on the door and opened it without waiting for Summer to answer. Sure enough, Blanche was seated on one end of Summer's couch, holding a cup of tea and looking at it as though wondering what it was doing in her hands.

"What do you mean, Douglas is arrested?" she was demanding of Summer.

Abby quickly joined them, shaking off Summer's questioning glance at the teapot.

"I don't know anything more than that," Summer said. "Jenny got a phone call from him. She said he was arrested and then she shooed us out her door."

"She did stop to call a lawyer for him," added Abby, realizing she had arrived too late to see Blanche's reaction when she first heard the news.

Blanche swung around to face Abby. She seemed not to have noticed her arrival. "But Douglas isn't a murderer," she said. "Why are they arresting him?" It sounded odd, coming from a woman who had spent the last five years believing he had killed her daughter.

"We don't know he didn't do it," said Abby, ignoring Summer's frown. "We don't even know for sure he didn't kill Laura."

"Of course he didn't kill Laura. Trevor did. She said so in her letter." It was difficult to convince someone a person couldn't say, 'that's the person who killed me' when she wasn't dead yet, so Abby didn't try.

"He didn't kill Trevor either," said Blanche in a softer voice. "I know he didn't because I did."

"What?" was the simultaneous reaction.

Blanche set down the untried cup of tea and reached for her tissue package. *The woman must buy them by the gross.*

After blowing her nose, Blanche went on. "After I left the message in Jenny's mailbox, I decided to look for her."

"She didn't seem to want to be found. She never confided in anyone—even where she worked," said Summer. "I was her next door neighbor and looked after her cat and even I didn't know where she worked."

"Actually, it was quite easy," said Blanche.

Abby and Summer both gave her an appraising look. Blanche must have hidden depths—at least at sleuthing.

"Her car was still parked in the lot. She must have left with someone else. So, I looked at the cars and they all had their condo number on their parking spot." *Not a great security feature on the part of the strata,* thought Abby. *They shouldn't be unidentifiable.*

"On the seat," said Blanche, "was an envelope—empty, I think, because it was torn, but it had a return address on it. The address was a moving company, so I figured it was a pay envelope or something, since she had no other reason to have it. The name was different, but then I knew she was using a fake name." Another sniffle, another reach for the tissue. "I went to the company and told the girl at the desk I was her mother and wanted to see her for a moment. She told me Patsy—since the envelope was addressed to her under that name, I used it—didn't come in that day. She had no idea where she was.

"I thought I had reached a dead end, but as I got into my car, a woman came out—not the one at the desk, but a different one. She acted all furtive and asked if I was really Patsy's mother. Of course I said yes and acted really distressed that I couldn't find her." She stopped as if to rethink her last sentence. "It wasn't an act. I *was* distressed. Anyway, she said she'd promised to keep it a secret where Patsy was, but she guessed she could tell her mother. She gave me directions to the trailer camp on Quadra and even which lot it was on."

She seemed to stop there. "Go on," prompted Summer.

"Well, I took the next ferry and finally found the trailer park—they really need better signage—and parked my car just outside the entrance. I found the right slot and knocked on the door. It flung open, but instead of Jenny or Douglas like I was expecting, it was Trevor!

"He looked as surprised as I was, but then he totally changed his expression and started to grin. He said something like, 'well, well, if it isn't Mama come to sort out her chicks.' Then he looked down and saw the letter I was holding. He snatched it out of my hand without a 'by your leave' or anything, but that was Trevor all along—charming when he wanted to be and downright rude and vicious when he pleased."

"I wonder how he found out where Jenny was staying?" asked Abby as Blanche paused for breath.

"I never had a chance to ask him," Blanche replied with a twisted sort of grimace that might pass for a grin. "He read the letter and crumpled it up. He threw it on the table and it landed in an empty cup. Then he asked me what I proposed to do about it. I told him I was going to the police after I'd talked to Douglas first. He laughed and began to talk about Laura. He told me how he was her lover and she had been such an easy lay—she was just begging him for it." Blanche stumbled over the words as though, by uttering them, she was somehow giving credence to them. "I got so angry, I yelled at him to shut up. He wouldn't. He just started saying more foul things about Laura and I couldn't stand to hear anymore. There was a wine bottle sitting on the table. I grabbed it and swung it at Trevor. He was so surprised he didn't even duck. He fell backwards and hit his head on the corner of the countertop by the sink. Then he didn't move. I ran out as fast as I could and drove around for a while trying to decide what to do. I couldn't make up my mind, so I just took the next ferry back. I guess I hoped they'd think it was an intruder who killed him." She stopped and reached for her keys. "But now that they've arrested Douglas, I can't stay quiet. I can't let someone else go to jail for what I did." She stood and wavered slightly, off balance.

"Whoa," said Abby. "I don't think you're in any shape to drive. Let one of us, or both, take you."

"No thanks. I'm quite all right. I'll be fine. It's something I have to do by myself."

Nothing they could say would shake her. She left without a backward glance and they watched from the doorway as she backed her car and turned its nose towards the exit. They were turning to go back inside when they heard a crash.

They ran to the entrance gates where Blanche's car sat, nose into a pillar. She sat in the driver's seat, head down, sobbing into her hands.

Abby knocked on the car window and pulled at the handle to open the door. Blanche looked up, tears streaming down her face. "I guess you were right," she said, sitting upright and injecting a quiet dignity into her voice. "I'd be grateful if one of you would drive me to the police station."

Abby took her elbow and helped her out. "What about your car? Should you call your insurance first?"

"It can wait."

"I'm just going to shift it out of the way," said Summer, reaching for Blanches' keys. As Abby guided Blanche back to the condo door, Summer moved the car to a visitor slot. "It doesn't look too damaged," she said when she returned "Just the bumper. You might want to fix it privately and not make a claim. No points against your license."

Blanche waved them off and said, "I'm not going to think

about it now. Can we go, please?"

They took Abby's car. She asked as they exited the complex, "Are we going to the local RCMP here or to the Quadra station?"

"Over there, please," said Blanche. "That's where they have Douglas?"

Neither Abby nor Summer knew, so they just went along with Blanche's wishes. Abby wasn't sure there was even a jail or holding cell on Quadra. It wouldn't really matter in the end.

As they waited in line for the ferry to load, a thought struck Abby. "The letter," she said to Blanche. "Did you pick it up?"

"No," she said. "I was so flustered, I just left it there. That's why I had to copy it out the best I could remember."

"The police must have it," said Summer. "They'd find it when they searched the trailer."

"If that's the case," said Abby, "they already know about Trevor and his history with Jenny, Laura, and Douglas." She glanced at Blanche, but she didn't appear to even be listening.

They had a fifteen minute wait for the next ferry. They spent it in silence, each likely thinking along the same lines but no one willing to share their thoughts. Blanche sat in the front seat with Abby. Abby stole a glance or two at Summer in the back, but failed in her attempt to make eye contact in the rear view mirror.

Once on board, the silence felt less oppressive. The noise of the ferry and the movements of others around them provided distraction.

They shot up the hill away from the terminal and, in a few minutes, were parked in front of the RCMP station.

Abby stopped the car to give Blanche a moment to compose herself before her big revelation, but she apparently didn't need it. Blanche was the first out of the car. Abby and Summer trailed at her heels.

They hung back, not sure how involved they should be. Would Blanche want their company as emotional support, or would she view them as intruders, their role as chauffeurs over?

Blanche walked up to the intake counter and stood patiently in front of a tall, middle-aged woman who was on the telephone, seemingly in a one-way conversation. Her blonde, streaked hair was pulled back into a high bun, a few tendrils escaping onto her collar. She finally said, "I'll pass on that information. Thanks for calling," and hung up, her attention now on her visitor. Her expression remained calm and neutral as Blanche informed her she wanted to make a confession. "To what crime would that be, Madam?"

Her gaze flickered slightly when Blanche told her, but she merely asked for her name and pushed a button on her phone. She turned slightly to the side, her glance still holding them in her view over her shoulder as she spoke softly into the receiver.

Turning to them, she asked, "Are you all together?" At their nod, "Take a seat, please. Sergeant Weaver will be with you in a moment."

True to her prediction, he appeared after a two or three minute eternity. Abby's original impression of him as a feline predator hadn't changed. His eyes were in motion, as though taking a video impression of them all, and again, the slight quiver to his moustache suggested a cat zeroing in on a kill. She would hate to be in Blanche's shoes.

His glance took in all three women but centered on Blanche. "Mrs. Covington?" She nodded. "Would you come with me, please?"

As she stood to follow him, he turned his attention to her companions. "If you two ladies would mind waiting? I may want to speak with you as well."

That solved the problem of what they should do next. Abby turned to Summer and said in a low voice, designed to bypass the ears of the keeper of the gate, "Do you think Douglas is still here? How can we find out?"

An interested look from the dispatcher closed off any reply Summer was going to make. There would be no privacy here for anything they might say, so it was best to remain silent. She wished they could have simply left Blanche and gone for coffee or a drive—somewhere they could talk without being overheard. Anything they said here was bound to be reported back to Weaver. It would look rather obvious if they left their chairs in front of the desk and moved to the far side of the room. It would rank in Ms. Calm and Cool's books as suspicious behavior.

So they waited. And waited. Eventually, Sergeant Weaver

reappeared. He dropped some papers off with Ms. C and C and leaned close to her ear, apparently giving instructions of some sort.

"Mrs. Covington is going to be tied up for a little longer," he said, as he turned to them. "Would you like to go for an hour, maybe have some coffee, and come back?" His face actually cracked into a smile, chasing away all feline comparisons Abby had felt.

"Does that mean we can take her home? Should we be calling a lawyer for her?" *Why didn't they do that before she confessed? Because it was up to Blanche to think of that?*

"I'll see you in an hour," he said. The smile had disappeared. Apparently, he didn't like answering questions, only asking them.

Abby stood quickly as he turned, resisting the impulse to make a rude gesture at his back. *Not a time to be juvenile, Abby.*

Chapter Sixteen

Back in the car, Abby turned to Summer. "Where to?" The Unicorn didn't appear to be the place to sit for an hour over a cup of coffee.

"There's a little cafe where we were shopping the other day. Let's go there."

"You'll have to give me directions. Which turn do we take?"

"You always were directionally challenged, weren't you? Just take the curve to the right here and drive straight on till we get there."

The coffee shop was at the near end of the complex, right beside the little bakery. The smell of fresh bread made Abby realize her lunch had been a rather tasteless scone. Her stomach rumbled and she promised it she'd take care of it as soon as they were inside.

They chose a table and realized they needed to make their order at the counter at the back of the shop. The display case, which took up most of the space, held a variety of goodies, most of them from the bakery next door, Abby thought.

Summer ordered a peppermint tea and an oatmeal cookie. Abby scanned the menu and thought maybe she should have something nutritional, like a salad or a bowl of soup.

But the scents coming from the cabinet and wafting in from the adjoining bakery as the front door opened and closed cinched the deal. "I'll have a slice of that red velvet cake and a cup of coffee, black," she told the teenage cashier. Surely the black coffee compensated somewhat for the cake?

Abby devoured the cake in a few large mouthfuls and instantly regretted her action. The cake was delicious, but the frosting was so sweet that it left a sickly aftertaste in her mouth. Abby's taste buds usually thanked her for any sweetness sent their way, but this had been overload. She made a face, swigged a large gulp of coffee, and looked up to see Summer grinning at her, a barely nibbled cookie in her hand.

"What?"

"You always were a Greedy Gus when it came to sweets, weren't you?"

"All right," Abby answered crossly. "I should have had the salad. I know. But it looked so good. Now it's going to just sit there, reminding me of my gluttony."

"Well, you can make up for it later," said Summer. "Have something boring and nutritious for dinner. Now let's try to figure out what's going on."

"I thought we knew. Blanche killed Trevor in a fit of rage and Douglas is innocent. They'll let him go, Blanche will get sympathy from any judge or jury and likely not get too long a sentence, and we..." She finished with a triumphant note in her voice. "We can go back to normal."

"I'm not so sure," said Summer. "If it's as clear cut as that, they would simply arrest Blanche."

"What makes you think they haven't?"

"The fact that he asked us to come back."

Abby sighed. "You're right," she said. "There's something going on that we don't know about. Let's go back and find out."

"Not yet," said Summer as Abby began to scrape her chair back. "It's only been fifteen minutes. Sergeant What's-His-Face said an hour."

"Weaver," said Abby.

"Hmmm?"

"Weaver is the sergeant's name. Just use a mnemonic device to remember. That's what I do."

"What do you use for Weaver?"

"I tried to picture him at a loom at first, but then had a better one. I just think about his receding hairline and then picture him with a full weave topping his head. Then I remember Weaver!"

Summer broke into a laugh and, seeing the occupants of the table at the back all turn to look, she clamped a hand over her mouth. "That works for me," she said. "Except now I'm going to picture him that way and laugh when I meet him again. Not a great way to inspire confidence in the local fuzz."

"Nobody calls them that anymore."

"Calls them what?"

"The police. No one calls them fuzz these days. You're not tying yourself to trees now in front of logging trucks and chainsaws."

Summer looked thoughtful. "Maybe I should be," she said. "You know, I've become an environmental sloth lately. Well, pretty much ever since I married Jack. I let myself become this storybook wife and mother and lost most of my social consciousness. Maybe it's time to go back to my activism."

"Don't be silly," said Abby. "You know what's bringing this on, don't you?"

"No, but I'm sure you'll tell me."

"With Jack gone and Jennifer flown the coop, you're trying to redefine your life. But that doesn't necessarily mean going back to being a hippie activist. It could mean looking at a whole new way to feel useful. You said something about volunteer work. Maybe expand that so you feel you're making a difference. Lots easier on the joints and muscles than becoming an eco-warrior and hanging out living in trees."

Summer reached across the table and gave her arm a slap. "I don't necessarily agree with your reasoning, but I do get the point about the aging joints. I could put a lot more energy into my volunteer work, or perhaps start a group on my own."

Summer sat motionless, apparently lost in thought. Abby waited a full minute before bringing her out of her reverie.

"I can't sit here a minute longer, just wondering what's going on." She matched her words to action and grabbed her purse and keys. "Coming?"

Summer followed her lead. "Let's drive by the trailer park

first and see if the police tape is still up everywhere. If we go back now, we'll just sit and wait. Besides, Blanche has my cell number and will call if she needs us."

Anything was better than sitting somewhere, waiting, whether the cafe or the police station, so Abby turned the car in the direction of the park. Or at least she thought so.

"Not this way," said Summer. "You need to turn right at the fork. Don't you remember?"

"Should have brought your car," grumbled Abby as she backed into a lane and reversed. "Next time, tell me before I make a wrong turn, not after."

They slowed as they came to the turn-off to the trailer park. Abby's car bumped over the gravelled but lumpy entrance, and they made the left turn to the row that held Jenny's trailer. There was no sign of police tape except for a circlet around one tall tree that managed to evade the cleaning up.

"Look," said Abby. "Whose car is beside the trailer? Is that Jenny's?" She pointed to an older model grey Taurus with a large dent on the front bumper and some old-looking scratches along the fender.

"No. It must be the one belonging to her friend. I guess the police brought it back after they picked up Douglas."

"But wouldn't they be going over it for evidence?"

"How would I know? I'm the eco-warrior, not the police confidante, remember?" Abby thought she had ruffled Summer's feathers a little if she was still going on about her activist comments earlier.

Suddenly, Summer clamped her hand onto Abby's wrist. "Turn around. Let's get out of here!"

Under Summer's insistence, Abby obeyed quickly. She reversed and was out on the main road before she stopped and turned to Summer. "What was that all about?"

"I saw someone moving about in the trailer. I didn't want to be caught snooping."

"If we saw them, it's a good chance they saw us. Do you think it was the police?"

"No. they wouldn't be there if the tape is down. It must be Jenny. She already thinks we're nosy. We don't need to add to her impression."

Abby bit her lip to stop asking just whose idea it had

been to come to the trailer.

She turned, the right direction this time, and pulled into the police station lot. Abby stood outside the car, waiting as Summer fiddled with her phone. The weather had cooled considerably and there was a hint of moisture in the air. The fluffy innocent clouds of that morning had firmed up and were moving across the sky as though in a hurry to make an important appointment. Rain was on the menu.

Summer finally exited the car, thrust her cell phone back into her purse, and said, "Are you going to stand there all day?" No comment about who she was texting. She wasn't mellowing. Abby hoped she hadn't hurt her feelings earlier, but she remembered back in college days. Summer often got into a tizzy about something and it never lasted long. This would pass. Come to think of it, Abby hadn't been her sunniest self today either. Maybe there was something in the air.

Chapter Seventeen

They chose seats farthest away from the dispatcher this time. They needn't have bothered. In a few minutes, Weaver came striding towards them. "Ah, there you are," he said, as though they were lost strays. "Mrs. Covington is just signing some documents for us and she'll be with you in a moment."

"So she's free to go?" said Abby at the same time as Summer said, "Should she have a lawyer?"

He didn't answer. Instead, he turned to the sound of footsteps down the hall as Blanche appeared.

Weaver put his hand to his head, then dropped it as though he had been going to lift a nonexistent hat, and disappeared back the way he'd come.

Abby and Summer both had their mouths opened to begin questioning Blanche, but she forestalled them, saying, "Let's get out of here. I've had enough of this place."

They trooped out to the car and Abby started the motor, not sure where she should be going. "Head to the ferry?" she asked Summer.

Summer turned her wrist over and wrinkled her nose. "Last one left not that long ago. It's nearly an hour till the next one, but we might as well wait in line there as anywhere."

Abby concurred and turned the car in the correct direction without instructions. Maybe this directionally challenged thing could be worked out, she thought.

They pulled into the waiting line at the terminal. No other cars were in front of them, but the odd foot passenger wandered around, apparently looking for ways to kill time. A woman walked along the terminal building, holding the leashes of two very active dogs, some sort of terriers, Abby supposed.

Abby and Summer both turned to Blanche, who had opted to sit in the back, probably as a way of trying to isolate herself from their questions. It wasn't going to work. Abby felt justified in having her curiosity slaked. After all, they had brought Blanche over, had been privy to a murder confession, so they had an explanation coming, whether Blanche though so or not.

A car pulled in behind them, and another behind that. The ferry wouldn't be too long coming.

Abby and Summer exchanged glances and Summer nodded. She would be the questioner.

She twisted in her seat to face Blanche. "Have you contacted a lawyer?" she began. The hard questions could wait.

Blanche shook her head. "I'll talk to someone later, but I'm not sure if they are going to lay any charges against me or not."

Another exchange of glances. No charges for murder? Still, they should have seen to it she had legal advice. Their bad for not insisting before she confessed.

"Apparently, I didn't kill him." She gave a little half smile. "I hit him with the wine bottle and he fell. I went into panic mode when he didn't move and I ran away. But, it turns out, he wasn't dead, just stunned. According to their medical report, the blow from the bottle wouldn't have killed much more than a large fly—and that's a quote," she said, offering up her first smile. "He did hit his head on the corner of the counter as he fell and that dazed him, but it was a knife wound that actually killed him. And they don't think I did that part of the attack."

Well, that's one for the books.

"So are they still holding Douglas?"

"They never were. Or at least not when I was there. He wasn't arrested, just brought in for questioning. I guess they didn't have enough to go on, so they let him go, just like me."

"So you weren't charged with anything?" Abby asked. "Not even assault?"

"Not yet," she said. "After they get it all sorted, there might be something, but I'm not going to worry about that now. I'm just so relieved that I didn't kill him." She hesitated a pause before adding, "Even if he did deserve it."

"Did they say why they didn't hold Douglas?"

"They weren't exactly confiding in me, you know," said Blanche a little testily. "But I did keep my ears open. Apparently, they found the knife behind the trailer and it was wiped clean of prints. The wine bottle still had mine on it, so that's partly why they thought it wasn't me since I didn't wipe my prints off everywhere else."

"Everywhere else?"

"Well, the doorknob, I guess. I had to leave my fingerprints and they matched the bottle and the door, but nothing else."

"I imagine Douglas and Jenny have their prints all over the place," said Abby. "So someone wiped only the prints on the knife. It must be someone who didn't touch anything else if those prints are still around."

"Not necessarily," said Summer. "It could be someone who didn't wipe the prints in other places because they could reasonably be expected to leave prints there." Both Abby and Summer studiously avoided meeting Blanche's eyes as they digested that thought.

"I don't know," said Blanche. "I'm only guessing a lot of this based on a word here and there. They weren't exactly filling me in. And yes, Douglas and Jenny would have their prints everywhere, but I wouldn't. And now, I don't want to talk about it anymore." She leaned back in her seat and closed her eyes, forestalling any further questions.

The ferry had docked by now and passengers and cars were heading up the hill to—wherever. It would be a lovely island to live on, thought Abby, but only if you worked there too. It would be a pain to have to take the ferry across twice a day to get to and from your job.

Then she thought about the letter. "Did you tell them about the letter?" she asked Blanche. "The one from Laura?"

Abby watched in the rear view mirror as Blanche's eyes

flickered open. "Of course I did," she said. Then she closed her eyes again.

The ferry ride across the passage was a silent one. Abby wondered about Douglas. Why had the police let him go? They mustn't think him guilty. Or maybe they just had no evidence and were waiting to build a case. Did they know about Denim Man too? What had Douglas or Jenny told them about him? Too many questions. And none of them were any of her business. She tried to repeat those words to herself like a mantra, but they wouldn't take hold. She and Summer had been drawn into this affair through no wrongdoing on their part—well, if you discounted a little housebreaking—and they deserved some answers.

The clouds had rumbled together in looming masses and the sea air was chilled as they docked. Tiny flecks of rain dotted the windshield as Abby turned the car onto the Island Highway.

"Where would you like to go now, Blanche?" Abby asked. "Do you want us to drop you off at your hotel?"

"No, thank you. I'd better pick up my car and see what the damage is. It should be still drivable, so I'll take it and get out of your hair."

She dug into her purse, probably looking for her keys. *She seems in a great hurry to get away from us*, thought Abby. Not that she could blame her.

"I want to stop off and talk to Douglas before I go. I still need to apologize to him for not believing him these last five years."

Abby slid a sideways glance at Summer. They hadn't told Blanche about their excursion to the trailer park, and their discovery that someone, probably Douglas and Jenny, were there. Oh well, Blanche would find out shortly that they weren't home and then be on her way. Past history wasn't their concern. It would sound lame to tell her what they knew and why. It was difficult having to constantly justify how you came by certain information. Curiosity was a trait not widely admired, especially by its targets.

As Abby pulled the Mazda into the visitor slot, the first thing that struck her was the grey, slightly battered Taurus parked on the other side of Blanche's car. It must be the one they saw at the trailer park. No way another vehicle would have that same dent in the bumper and scratches on the fender. The car hadn't been on the same ferry as them, she was pretty sure, but then they were first on and she might have missed spotting them. In that case, they must have taken a shortcut home. More likely they would have caught the earlier ferry if they left right after Abby and Summer had sped away from the trailer park.

She lifted her hand to gesture, but she could tell by the direction of Summer's gaze that she had noticed it too.

As they rounded the corner to the front entrances of the condos, Abby checked the assigned parking. Sure enough, Jenny's own car was there, so that meant she and Douglas must be home. The rain was beginning to pelt down now, but Blanche hunched her shoulders, pulling her head into her collar like a tortoise, and marched up to the walk to the neighboring condo.

Summer slid her key into her own front lock, Abby watching from behind her shoulder as Blanche walked over to Jenny's door and lifted the knocker. At least the overhang sheltered them from the rain.

Summer waited with her key in the lock. No answer came to Jenny's door. Blanche lifted the knocker again. Summer opened her door slowly, obviously not wanting to leave the step but aware that Blanche might consider her hesitation odd.

Finally, as Summer reluctantly entered and Abby was about to follow inside, Blanche looked over and said, "Looks like no one's home."

Abby didn't disabuse her. "Would you like to come over and wait?" She was sure Summer would forgive her for uttering invitations to her home.

"No thanks. I could leave a note." She seemed to consider, possibly remembering how little good it did her last time. "No, I'll come back later."

"Let's make sure your car is all right," said Abby. She followed her to the parking lot, wishing she had grabbed an umbrella, and waited as Blanche gave the car a once-over. "Nothing much," she said. "The fender is barely scratched and nothing is touching the tires. It's just a bumper issue." She jumped into the driver's seat as though anxious to get away. And who could blame her?

When Abby got back to Summer's, she pushed the front door open without knocking and was just leaning down to take off her shoes, damp and muddy from the rain.

"I'm in here," called Summer from the living room. "Kettle is nearly boiling."

"Never mind the kettle," hissed Abby in a loud whisper. "Get out here." For just as she was about to close the front door behind her, a figure walked up the path and headed towards next door. He wore jeans and a denim jacket, and slouched against the rain, hands in pockets, no outer coat or hat for protection.

Denim Man! Summer quickly joined her and they stood just inside the doorway, peering out, held open a crack to watch as he knocked. If they didn't answer to Blanche, they certainly wouldn't to Denim Man.

He knocked a second and a third time, the last without benefit of the knocker, merely banging his fist on the door. He twisted the doorknob, but it didn't give. His eyes swung from one side of the entry to the other, picking up the movement of Summer's door, open a scant inch or two.

He took a few steps in their direction. Abby was about to pull the door shut, not wanting a confrontation. Summer had a different plan. She pushed the door widely open and said to the approaching man in a clear, loud voice, "Can we help you?"

"Friends of theirs, are you?" he asked with a smile that more closely resembled a sneer.

"What do you want?" asked Summer as Abby joined her on the outer step. *Safety in numbers.*

"None of your business," he said. "But you can pass on a message."

"Go ahead," said Summer. "Would you like me to write it down?"

"No need. Just tell Martindale he has forty-eight hours."

"Forty-eight hours for what?"

"He'll know. Tell him." The "or else" was definitely implied in the message.

With that, he reversed direction and, after a few nonchalant steps that appeared designed for effect, broke into a jog against the pouring rain.

Chapter Eighteen

"Well!" was Abby's first reaction as they watched him all the way to the parking lot. Then, "You had me worried for a moment. He didn't look like a character you'd want to have a row with."

"Typical bully," said Summer. "He'd only attack you in a dark alley with no witnesses, and only if you were smaller than him."

"Well, we are," was Abby's practical response.

"Yes, but there are two of us. And besides, we served a purpose for him. He had no reason to harm us."

"Douglas and Jenny might be a different matter. I wonder what the forty-eight hours is about."

They had remained standing on the step, leaning back from the rain under the overhang, watching as Denim Man peeled out of the drive, but it was chilly in the wind and they turned to go back inside. Abby saw a flicker of movement just as they re-entered.

Back inside, she said to Summer in a whisper, "I just saw the blinds move on the window next door."

"Why are you whispering? No one can hear us."

"Oh, right. Well, they are home, definitely. Should we call them?"

"Let's go over instead. Maybe they'll open the door to us,

where they wouldn't to Blanche or Denim Man."

Just then the phone rang. Summer followed the ring to find the phone on the coffee table, and made hand motions towards Abby as she answered. The gestures were incomprehensible to Abby, but she soon picked up on the fact that it was Jenny on the other end.

Summer hung up and said, "Well, we have a royal summons to attend next door. Jenny wants to know what he said to us."

"What are we waiting for?"

They took the shortcut across the grass at a run, but were still drenched when they were admitted to Jenny's foyer. They slipped off their shoes and brushed fruitlessly at their clothing to dislodge the rain droplets.

No offer of tea or coffee, but they were ushered into the inner sanctum of the living room where Douglas sat leaning forward in a recliner with an empty cup and plate on a side table. Another plate sat on the coffee table with a half sandwich and a crumpled serviette.

Abby and Summer sat side by side on the couch with Jenny across from them in the big matching chair and Douglas off to the side, out of the line of direct eye contact.

"What did he want?" asked Jenny without preamble.

Abby settled on the straight answer. "He said to tell Douglas he had forty-eight hours," she said simply.

A quick exchange of looks between Jenny and Douglas. "Forty-eight hours for what?" Jenny asked.

"He didn't get specific. The assumption seemed to be that Douglas would know what he was talking about."

"Look," cut in Summer, "we've become involved in your saga through no fault of our own. We've worried when you disappeared, looked after Peaches when we didn't know where you were, found a dead body in your trailer, and kept you company in a police station. Now we're passing on messages from thugs. Don't you think we deserve the truth?" She stared straight at Jenny without blinking or wavering, as though attempting a mind meld.

Finally, Jenny shifted her gaze downwards and said, "You're right. You know most of the story anyhow. You know Douglas spent four years in jail for killing his wife. You also know he didn't do it—that it was Trevor who killed Laura."

Not entirely convinced on that one yet. "Douglas can tell you better than I can." She looked across at her brother, who straightened and obeyed her directive.

"In prison, you get to know a lot of bad people. You basically have to learn to get on with them without getting too involved, if you know what I mean." Abby didn't, but she wasn't going to interrupt when they finally were getting to the truth.

"Well, when I was released from jail, I was given an envelope to pass on to someone. The problem was, I didn't realize it at the time. The janitor bumped into me when I was heading out, after I'd picked up my personals and been cleared. I didn't know until I was on the bus heading home that he had slipped it into my pocket. Even then, I didn't realize what it was. I thought it was something I'd dropped or —well, I don't know exactly what I thought. I was concentrating on getting home and trying to decide what to do next. Anyhow, when I got off the bus, I grabbed my jacket and the envelope must have fallen out. Then I got the phone calls, telling me what to do with it."

"What was in it? Money?"

"In an indirect way. It was a list of names, I think, although I'm not entirely sure, worth a lot in the right hands. I guess they figured I'd be able to pass them on. No worries about mail censorship or visitors frisked on the way out. Or maybe it was just a ploy to get me roped in to work with them. Who knows? Anyhow, I didn't have it anymore and I told them so. I wasn't about to put in a request to lost and found at the bus service. I'd go back inside just having possession of illegal stuff. I didn't answer the phone at first, but then I started seeing cars and people outside my house, watching me. So finally I answered the phone and told them what happened. They didn't believe me." He stopped for breath, picked up his cup, and realized it was empty. He seemed to have lost the impetus to go on.

Jenny picked up from there. "So Douglas left his car there so he wouldn't be followed and took a bus up here. He thought no one knew where he was heading, but, somehow, they must have tracked him. Or maybe they knew where I was all along." She picked up the serviette and twisted it in her hand before dumping it back on the half-eaten sandwich.

She gave a rueful smile. "I spent all that time and effort hiding and it doesn't seem to have done much good. They found me. Trevor found me—and he's the one I was hiding from in the first place."

Abby waited for her to go on, but, like Douglas, she seemed to have run out of steam.

"So this Denim Man," she prompted—they seemed to know who she was talking about—"did you tell the police about him?"

Douglas looked up. "No. I didn't know about him, not specifically, that is. Jenny told me someone had been snooping around, but that wasn't until after I was let go by the police. We went over to Quadra as an added security in case someone followed. Didn't do much good." He lapsed back into silence.

Abby thought back. That was right. It was she and Summer who had told Jenny about Peaches getting out and about Blanche and Denim Man. And that was after they found Trevor's body.

"Don't you think they should know?" A glance between brother and sister.

"Yes," said Jenny, directing her comments towards Douglas. "They should know. We don't have to tell them about the letter, just that someone was snooping around and in the house. It means someone else was here. If he went looking for you at the trailer, he could have thought you were Trevor. Or Trevor was you."

"I think you're going to have to tell them about the letter too. That's what gives someone else a motive. If they thought Trevor was Douglas, that is." Abby couldn't understand why the reluctance to give the police information that might help Douglas, but then his time in prison for a crime he might not have committed could alter his attitude to parting with information to authority.

Jenny stood up. They knew it was a signal they should leave. They did. Jenny didn't follow them to the front door or bid goodbye as they donned their damp shoes.

The rain was beginning to let up when they crossed to Summer's door. "Want to come in?" she asked.

"No. I think it's time I headed home. I've had enough of that pair for today. Let's have coffee tomorrow and compare notes. Maybe we'll have figured something out by then. Or," she corrected, "maybe the police will have it figured out by then."

"Don't you have classes tomorrow?"

"Just one early one. I'll be home by ten and come over then."

Abby was met by a neglected ball of fur when she pushed open her own front door. "Sorry, Ajax, but I know you're not starving, and you do have some of the hard stuff there. It's too early for dinner."

Ajax didn't agree, but she fobbed him off with a treat. Her pants and shirt were damp from the rain and her bones felt chilled. A hot bath and a change were called for.

Ajax followed her to the bathroom and sat on the mat, front paws tucked tidily underneath him while she ran the water. His expression seemed to ask why humans would willfully get wet, but then, if the food dish was kept replenished, why worry?

She stripped and eased into the hot water with a contented sigh. Heaven was a hot bath with lavender and rosemary salts. Her bones began to warm up and she tried to put today out of her mind. *Think of something totally mundane*, she thought. *Fill your mind with detail and there will be no room for murder.* She began to plan her shopping list, but that made her stomach rumble and she realized Ajax was right. It was time for dinner.

She heaved out of the tub and decided it was a sloth day. Instead of redressing in dry day clothes, she opted for pajamas and a dressing gown. She dearly hoped no one would knock on her door, forcing herself to answer in her relaxed state. But, who would knock? Not Summer, and Mandy was long gone. She hadn't made a batch of new friends here yet. And why should she care what a salesman or pamphlet leaver would think?

She opened the fridge door and stared inside. Hmmm. Leftover chicken. She had romaine lettuce and bottled dressing, so a makeshift chicken Caesar would go well, especially with the remains of the bottle of wine that stared back at her.

She would eat dinner in the living room in front of the TV and watch some of the many programs she'd PVR'd but not yet viewed. She knew she had at least two unwatched episodes of her favorite mystery, *Midsomer Murders*. She re-thought that; no murder tonight. Instead, she'd watch the last *Big Bang Theory*.

She began to throw together a salad.

Ajax circled her ankles. She knew she shouldn't, but she dropped a small piece of chicken on the floor for him. He already had the begging habit; she was merely reinforcing it.

She had just started to relax, her salad finished and the wine half done, when her phone rang. She picked it up quickly and was pleased to see Mandy's number on call display. Pleased and nervous. While she always loved Mandy's calls, the little niggle worry at the back of her mind immediately asked the question, "What's wrong?"

Nothing, it turned out was the answer.

"I just wanted to make sure you weren't getting over your head in this murder thing," Mandy said.

"Murder thing? What a strange way to put it. No, I'm staying out of it." She crossed her fingers as she thought of her confrontation with Denim Man, driving Blanche to make a confession, and passing on cryptic messages to Douglas. That wasn't really getting involved. Not over her head anyhow.

Mandy knew better. "Mom! What have you and Summer been doing?"

Abby held out as long as she could, but, even over the phone, Mandy could turn the thumbscrews.

She told her about Blanche's confession, which turned out not to be a confession at all, and about Douglas and Blanche both being let go. She omitted Denim Man and the bit about the lost letter Douglas had received in jail. That smacked of organized crime and that would worry her daughter. It worried her.

When she finally said goodbye to Mandy, she poured herself a second glass of wine, pulled her laptop onto her knee, and checked her e-mails. Part of her hoped to see another e-mail from Neil. Most of her didn't. His absence left a hole in her heart, but when she thought back, most of her relationship with Neil was little bits between huge absences and that wasn't the kind of love affair she wanted, not at her age. That sent her mind to Richard. She wanted a relationship like the nearly thirty years she had with him—minus the infidelity, that is. She sighed and wondered, *Can you ever be sure of another person?*

She answered a few work-related e-mails and turned her attention to Facebook for distraction. Maybe a cat video would take her mind off broken relationships. Ajax jumped up beside her and pawed at the computer keyboard. "I guess I'll have to settle on you instead of cute cats on video," she said, ready to give up. But then her e-mail highlighted a new item.

When she realized who it was from, she dumped Ajax off her knee unceremoniously and riveted her gaze on the letter. It was a joint letter, to her, Mandy, and Richard. And it was from Matthew. *"Mom, Dad, Mandy, a new development in my career plan. I have an offer for a job in Victoria. It's with a humanitarian organization trying to provide medical care to third world countries. The difference is, I won't be travel-ling—well, I will travel, but my base will be there. I've decid-ed it's time to come home."*

It took a few minutes before Abby's eyes were dry enough to act. She wrote a joyful reply and sent it as a group e-mail. Apparently, Richard and Mandy weren't that far away from their mail either as letters began to fly back and forth.

She finally closed her computer and pulled Ajax onto her lap, holding him so tightly he squirmed and jumped off her knee. Matthew was coming home! Now he would be living only a few hours' drive away instead of halfway around the world. Now he would be safe. She quickly crossed her fingers at that thought; she didn't want to jinx anything.

She phoned Mandy again. Some feelings just couldn't be conveyed via e-mail. By the time she ended that call, she realized it was bedtime, but she couldn't sleep, not with all that excitement. Instead, she pulled out some old photo al-bums from when the kids were small. She flicked the pages, watching the growth of her two babies from a naked-on-the-rug age to their high school graduations. There weren't many recent pictures. Newer photos were all stored on disc or in a cloud somewhere. Looking at a slideshow didn't have the same magic as holding an album on your lap and running a finger over a memory.

She stopped at one photo of a picnic. She and Richard had taken the kids for a day at the lake. It was one of those unbeatable Manitoba autumn days. The leaves were intact but turning, the sun was still hot even though it left earlier in the evening, and it was too late in the year for pesky mosquitoes. They had set up a table at the campground and cooked hot dogs over the fire, leaving room for toasted marshmallows and then a stop for ice cream on the way home. How long ago it seemed! And yet—if she closed her eyes, she could still smell the campfire smoke. She could touch the sticky cheeks of her children, resplendent with streaks of cotton candy ice cream and dabs of marshmallow. And she could hold the hand of her husband as they watched a red and gold sunset. She gave a deep sigh and closed the album. She was happy then. She wondered if we are each allowed an allotted number of happy days and she had already spent hers. No! She wouldn't believe that. She had many more happy days ahead, especially now that her son was coming home.

On that note, she put the albums back in their cupboard and headed for her bed, Ajax following one step behind, like a consort behind his queen.

The happy dreams she anticipated didn't come. Instead, she fell almost immediately into a dreamless slumber that lasted until Ajax poked her cheek with a tabby paw, announcing it was time for breakfast.

Chapter Nineteen

Abby surfaced in the morning, aware of a feeling of contentment as she brushed away the orange paw swiping her cheek. Still in a half sleep, it took a few seconds to realize the reason for the bubbles of happiness that floated to her consciousness. Matthew was coming home!

She relished that thought, lost in plans, as she dressed, had breakfast, and attended to her cat's needs. When she finally glanced down at her wrist, she jumped so quickly into the present she startled Ajax into making a bee-line for the safety of the living room. She was going to be late!

She dumped the remains of her coffee and grabbed her purse and keys, holding the last piece of her toast in her mouth as she made her exit to the car.

For all her distraction, her morning class went well. Her students were used to each other now, and familiar enough with her to jump into discussion at the drop of a preposition. The course was nearly half over now, summer classes only lasting a few weeks, so Abby knew she had better get busy with plans for final tests and grades.

She was buckling her seatbelt to leave the college parking lot when her cell rang. Expecting a family member, she felt a stab of disappointment at the sound of Summer's voice.

"What's up?" she said, in lieu of "hello."

"Are you done for the day?"

"Yes," she said. "I was going to call you before I came over. And why are you whispering?"

"I'm not," said Summer, raising her voice fractionally. "But they're on the patio beside mine. At least they were a few minutes ago. I don't want to be overheard."

"On the patio? So they've finally decided to join the outside world again."

"No, they're still secluded, but now they're looking for Peaches. She escaped."

"Oh." As a fellow cat-lover, Abby immediately felt a stab of concern. "I hope she hasn't wandered too far. If she's not used to traffic..."

"She hasn't," said Summer, whispering again. "I have her."

"You've kidnapped Peaches?" Abby realized she had nearly shouted the question and looked guiltily around her to be sure no one had heard. Her end of the lot was empty.

"Sshhh. I haven't kidnapped her." Indignation raised her voice again. "Get over here and I'll tell you all about it."

With an invitation as filled with mystery as that, Abby lost no time arriving at Summer's door. She didn't stop to drop off her overflowing briefcase, filled with unmarked papers, at home.

Summer yanked Abby in from the step as though she was a spy on the run. She quickly closed the door, then glanced furtively back towards the living room where curtains were pulled across the patio doors. Now who was hiding out?

Sure enough, there was Peaches, sitting quite at home on a kitchen chair, licking her lips to remove remnants of whatever offering she had received from her kidnapper.

Summer sat in one of the kitchen chairs, and Abby followed suit. "What in the world is going on?"

"I heard Jenny and Douglas last night yelling at each other. These condo walls aren't as well insulated as they should be. I could hear well enough to know they were arguing, but not well enough to make out what they were saying." She paused for breath, and absent-mindedly reached out a hand to pat Peaches, pulling it back when she realized what allergens would be sitting on that lovely coat.

"Anyhow, I did make out the words 'Trevor' and 'police,' but nothing more."

"That's not surprising, is it? Of course Trevor's death is top of their minds, until the police find out who killed him."

"It was more than that, I'm sure. I've never heard them fight before."

"And where does Peaches come into all this?" Abby gave her a rub under the chin and the cat began a loud purr.

"She got out this morning. Jenny phoned to see if she had come here."

"So you lied. Why?"

"I didn't lie. At that time, I hadn't seen her. I looked out my door just before I called you and there she was. I brought her in and closed the curtains so no one could see in."

"Are you going to tell me why you turned into a cat-napper?"

"It's obvious, isn't it? Jenny and Douglas won't let anyone in to talk to them. They've gone back to their seclusion. The only reason they let us in yesterday was to see what Denim Man had said. So, this is our in."

"What do you mean, 'our'? It doesn't take two people to return a cat. Won't she think it strange when we both appear on the doorstep?"

"Maybe, but I think it's best as a two-man job. She's not going to chuck us both out. We go through the patio with Peaches, I tell her how she showed up at my door, and when she reaches out to get Peaches from me, you slip into the room. She turns, I follow. She's not going to physically remove us, no matter how much she wants us gone. It's only good manners to thank us for returning her cat."

"And what then? Just because we're in her home doesn't mean she's going to confide in us. And Douglas even more so. They'll say their thanks and break into a stony silence till we leave."

"That's where the two of us come in. We can make a conversation go between us until they have to say something. Now, grab the cat and let's go."

Abby complied, although her inner voice was telling her this was insane and what business of theirs was this anyhow? The police would figure it out in their own good time and they could go back to life as it was and should be.

It only took seconds after their knock for Jenny to slide open the patio doors. Abby saw the relief on her face at Peaches' safe return and felt guilty over their duplicity. As Jenny reached out for Peaches and began crooning to her in that way only cat owners did, she felt Summer give her a nudge in the ribs. Reluctantly, she slid past Jenny and Peaches to stand just inside the doorway. Summer followed as Jenny turned to face Abby.

Sure enough, Jenny frowned briefly, but clamped a smile on top of the frown as she thanked them for finding Peaches. There was no sign of Douglas.

By now, Summer had followed Abby inside and advanced to the center of the room. As she was about to declare residency by sitting on the couch, Jenny said, "Let's go to the kitchen. I think there's coffee left." She led the way, still holding her cat. It was obvious she wasn't welcoming their presence, but, as Summer correctly guessed, she wasn't going to throw them out on their ear after finding her beloved pet.

Once in the kitchen, Peaches decided she'd had welcome enough and squirmed out of Jenny's grasp. She headed straight for her food dish. Abby and Summer sat at the kitchen table as Jenny poured coffee into two mugs. She apparently wasn't going to join them—point taken and recognized. Abby took a tentative sip at her half-filled mug. It was super strong and she choked slightly as she inhaled coffee.

"Sorry," she gasped. "Shouldn't drink and breathe at the same time." She spotted a box of tissues on the kitchen counter. She quickly crossed to the counter and pulled tissues from the box, dabbing at her eyes. "Sorry," she began again. The rest of the sentence died in her throat as she glanced down at a letter protruding from under the box.

It seemed to have been thrust under the tissue box and Abby had dislodged it.

A shock of recognition ran through her, stiffening her back and stopping her words. For the dirty and creased envelope on the counter had Blanche Covington's name and address written across the front. A dark brown smudge obliterated the last part of the postal code. It could only be the letter Douglas had mailed to Blanche, the one that had convinced her that Trevor had killed her daughter. But Blanche had left the letter in the trailer, and if the police hadn't found it there, it could only mean one thing. Trevor's killer had picked it up. And that meant Trevor's killer was either Jenny or Douglas. But it couldn't be Jenny; she had been with them, and before that at the store.

Abby knew she had been standing there too long, mesmerized by the letter and its implications.

She was aware of silence in the room. No conversation was coming from the table—no inquisition led by Summer. She tried to force herself to turn around, but she couldn't move. Then she heard footsteps behind her and a gasp from the direction of the table.

Chapter Twenty

"You just couldn't let it go, could you?" came the distinctively masculine voice behind her. "Any normal person would have gone about their own business and not stuck her nose into ours."

She forced herself to turn. She expected to see Douglas standing behind her. What she didn't expect was the gun in his hand. Where had it come from? How would Douglas, a convicted felon, own a gun? A glance at Jenny gave her the answer. Jenny had the gun to protect herself from Trevor. In that brief glance, she realized Jenny was as shocked at the scene before her as Summer and Abby were.

She turned her eyes back to Douglas. He didn't look angry. He didn't look threatening. Instead, he looked—resigned. Resigned and almost apologetic.

"Douglas, don't," came the response from Jenny. "Don't make things worse."

"How could they possibly get worse?" he said. "Four years in prison for something I didn't do, now they're going to put me back. I can't let that happen."

Abby waited for more remonstrance from Jenny, but she had lapsed into silence. She tried to keep her voice low and calm. "Douglas, they will look at the extenuating circumstances. When they know you didn't kill Laura, it will make a difference. And killing Trevor—surely they'll consider self-defense or something else in your favor. Jenny's right. Don't make this worse than it has to be."

"A legal expert, are you?" Douglas forced out a crooked smile that suddenly added to the threat of the situation. "I have to get away from here. I have to disappear."

"No, Douglas. Please don't. Look at me, Douglas." Jenny's eyes were full of tears as she tried to force her brother to give her his attention.

Abby watched Douglas as warring expressions flickered across his face. Guilt, sorrow, resentment, fear, and now she realized the anger was there too.

Abby said, "What are you going to do? Hurting us won't make it go away. Everything you've done till now can be dealt with. But if you shoot us, that's a totally different matter."

Douglas gave a start as though he had received a shock. He looked down at the gun as though it was an unknown object that had jumped into his hand. "Shoot you? I wasn't going..." Then he suddenly changed tack. "If you want to stay alive, you'll do as I say. Jenny is going to tie you up."

"No, Jenny isn't." Douglas swung around to face his sister. She locked onto his gaze. "This is going to stop now, Douglas. We've both lived through too much to want to make it worse. Running will only be a temporary solution. Hurting them? I know you can't do that. Give me the gun. Then I'm going to call the police. No, you're going to call them. It will look better that way."

For an endless moment, their gazes locked. Douglas finally lowered his eyes. A second later, he lowered the gun. His shoulders slumped and he reached for the back of a kitchen chair to steady himself. He dropped the gun on the table in front of his sister and fell into the chair, burying his head in his hands. Sobs shook his body.

Abby and Summer didn't move. They looked to Jenny, who put her arm around Douglas, comforting him as mother to child.

When Douglas finally straightened, he looked from one of them to the other and said, "I'm sorry. I never would have hurt you. I only wanted you to go away. I wanted everything to go away." He turned back to Jenny. "I'll make that phone call now."

They waited in an embarrassing silence for the police to arrive. How can you make small talk with someone who a few minutes ago pointed a gun at you and is waiting to make a confession to murder? It didn't matter to Jenny and Douglas. They seemed almost unaware of the presence of their visitors, lost in their own sorrows.

Abby could hear the ticking of the kitchen clock and the purr of a car leaving the parking area. Peaches came over to Jenny and, when ignored, leapt on Summer's lap. Summer patted her absently until she sneezed. At that point, Peaches gave up on them all and jumped down, stalked from the room, waving her tail on high.

When the police arrived, it wasn't Weaver and the men they had dealt with on Quadra. Even so, these unfamiliar officers seemed to know exactly what the issue was and took Douglas into custody with little fanfare. Jenny gave her brother a hug and said, "I'll call your lawyer. Don't say anything more until he sees you first." She aimed a look at the lead officer as though to emphasize the words. "Douglas will make a full statement *after* he talks to his lawyer." Then she turned to Abby and Summer. "I don't think you need to stay," she said. "You've done quite enough."

The police had a different opinion. "You will have to come and make a statement."

Abby sighed. She was spending as much time in police stations as in a classroom these days.

She and Summer took their respective cars to the station to fulfill their duty as witnesses. It promised to be a long day. Her stomach rumbled, protesting all it had seen that day in the line of food was a quick breakfast before rushing to class and a rancid cup of coffee here. She hoped there would be a chance to slide through a drive-through on the way to the police station.

Chapter
Twenty-One

After a couple of long, theory-filled, tea afternoons with Summer to discuss in endless detail their recent adventures, life slipped back into routine. Both Abby and Summer were waiting for stories in the newspaper, now their only source of information. Jenny had disappeared from view and the police appeared to have no further use for them.

The next two weeks were busy ones for Abby, with major papers to mark from her courses, a grant proposal to finish, and some networking to catch up on.

She also kept up a barrage of e-mails with her family, anticipating Matthew's return.

The last letter informed them Matthew would be coming home in two weeks. First he was going to make a stop in Manitoba to visit with his father. From there, he would fly to Victoria to find an apartment and get ready for his new job.

Summer phoned on a Saturday morning. "I've just made lemon bars," she said. "And we can have lemon-ginger tea to go with them. There's news," she added, in case Abby needed inducement to accept.

"I'll be there in fifteen minutes." Abby had tried to put the events from her mind with little success. Every time she immersed herself in work, Douglas and Jenny intruded into her thoughts. Maybe when she knew more, they would fade away and let her get on with her life. Even the advent of Matthew's arrival couldn't obliterate her curiosity.

Abby found a spot in the visitor's parking area and rounded the corner to the condo fronts. She stopped suddenly. Now she knew what Summer's piece of news would be. A moving van stood in front of Jenny's entrance. The back was open and two burly men were shoving bits and bobs of rugs and wrappers into the already loaded truck box. As Abby began to move again, one shouted something to the other and pulled the doors shut. The other man nodded and made his way, whistling, to the passenger door.

The tantalizing scent of lemon met her in the doorway. Summer must have poured the kettle as she stood watching the movers.

"Did you see?" Obviously a rhetorical question, for how could she not see?

They both jumped backwards as the door next to them swung open. They watched through the barest of cracks as Jenny exited her house and, without a backward glance, placed a cat carrier and purse into her car and drove off, following the moving van.

"Well! I guess that's that." Abby was the first to speak. "I can't blame her for wanting to get away from here, after all that's happened."

"Neither can I. I imagine she'll want to be close to Douglas as he sorts out his situation."

"A murder charge is a little more than a situation," said Abby.

"But consider the circumstances. He spent years in jail for something he didn't do. Surely that will give him some leverage for this."

"You're probably right. And this won't be called murder. They'll dress it up in fancier terms, and if he has a good lawyer, he'll likely get a light sentence. A jury would be sympathetic. After all, the man he killed, killed his wife. At least, we think he did."

"Doubting Thomas," said Summer. "Of course Trevor killed Laura. I know you're going to say Jenny had me brainwashed, but it's not just her and Douglas. Blanche was convinced he was guilty too. And he as much as admitted it to her."

"Okay, okay. I'll agree with you. Let's just hope a jury will too. Douglas doesn't fit the bill of a cold-hearted murderer. Look how he couldn't make himself hurt us, even though we were between him and a jail cell. But now I imagine the only way we'll find out more is by watching the newspapers," sighed Abby.

"Not exactly," said Summer with a smug smile.

"What did you find out?"

"Jenny did come over to say goodbye and thank me for looking after Peaches for her."

"And you didn't think to call me?" Much as Abby had been the one to try to distance herself from events, she felt indignant at being left out.

"I just did. She came over while the movers were loading. The police on Quadra found Denim Man. He had warrants outstanding for some other things, so he's going to be in jail, maybe longer than Douglas. Now that the police know about him and why he was after him, Douglas might be a witness for them. Oh, and apparently, the lost letter turned up. You'd never guess where."

"Where?"

"Lost and Found." Summer's triumphant expression suggested she had personally found the item.

"So, that covers all the loose ends. It's a relief to know it's all over. Now we can get back to normal."

"Speaking of normal, when is Matthew getting home?"

"He's going to visit Richard for a while first, so it will be nearly a month before he makes it to the island."

Abby drove home feeling a mix of emotions, satisfied to know Denim Man wouldn't be knocking on Summer's door, sympathy for Jenny and what still lay ahead, sympathy for Douglas too, for that matter. But a little part of her brain accused her of missing the excitement. Never mind, she had her own excitement to look forward to.

After a dinner from her list of healthy meals, Abby sat on the couch, legs pulled up under her, stroking Ajax as he lounged on the armrest beside her.

She opened her e-mail and there it was. Another letter from Neil. She thought she had closed that door by not replying to his last missive.

She hesitated only a moment before opening it.

"One last try, Abby. I think we still have places to go to-gether. How about we make San Francisco one of them? I'm off next week to California to deal with some contracts for Nikki. If you meet me there after I'm done, we can have a few days together to sort things out. Even if you decide it's goodbye, I think we should do it in person. What do you say?"

In one more week, Abby would be done her summer courses. Two weeks stretched between then and Matthew's arrival. She pictured Neil, as she had first seen him, en route to a Lake of the Woods island, lounging in the airport, an easy grin on his face, evasive lock of dirty blond hair tumbling across his forehead. Her heart gave a little somersault.

Before she could begin that endless conversation of pros and cons with herself that never led anywhere, Abby clicked onto a travel website. She selected a flight, punched in her dates, and reached for her purse to grab her credit card. There! It was done.

She went back to her e-mail and clicked reply. *"I'll be there next Friday, flight arrives at one p.m."*

She considered adding more information, but with a grin, decided she'd leave him to wonder. Didn't a little mystery add to romance?

About the Author

Sharon McGregor is a west coast transplant from the Canadian prairies, on a mission to escape the cold. Her imagination and story weaving got its start when she was an only child living on a farm. She's moved on from cowgirl dreams to romance and mystery, but hasn't lost her love for horses.

She writes humour, romance and cozies, sometimes a combination of all three. When not writing or reading, she is often found walking the dogs along the ocean. In spite of her attempts to escape winter, she loves watching her grandchildren at figure skating and hockey. The main item not yet ticked on her bucket list is travel. She wants to set her foot on six continents—she'll give Antarctica a pass, thank you.

Visit Sharon McGregor's web page and blog and sign up for her newsletter at:

www.sharonmcgregor.com

Visit her Facebook Author page at:

www.facebook.com/SharonMcGregorauthor/

www.ingramcontent.com/pod-product-compliance
Lightning Source LLC
Chambersburg PA
CBHW030543130626
46552CB00006B/2403